PRAISE FOR
THE MAGIC GOWN

"What an adventure (Lilly's travels in the Land of Ten Kings and Roses) is! The colorful illustrations are absolutely gorgeous."
—Dr. Tami Brady
TCM Reviews, April 4, 2008

". . . a lovely modern fairy tale! I loved the book. . . . gives young readers all sorts of positive messages about relationships, friendship, respect, manners, and doing the right thing. . . . a terrific book to use for bedtime stories (and) to further encourage young imaginations and creativity."
—Cheryl Nason
Dallas Book Diva
Interview April 8, 2008

"Children who venture into magical lands such as Oz, Narnia, or Wonderland will follow Lilly eagerly on her quest to find Princess Anais, wearer of the Magic Gown, and restore 'the tenth king' to his throne in The Land of Ten Kings and Roses. . . . (the author's) impressionistic watercolors recall Manet and Van Gogh, spilling indiscriminately throughout the book. . . ."
—Elizabeth Breau
ForeWord Magazine
September/October 2007

". . . a fantasy novel . . . to delight young readers . . . beautifully illustrated with . . . full-color paintings on virtually every page. Dragons, dreams, and destiny abound in this enchanting adventure by children's poetry and dream workshop leader J.L. Kimmel."
—*The Midwest Book Review*
July 2007

"*The Magic Gown* is a quality story about what has already come. . . . it is not only a magical adventure of transformation and hope but an inspirational reminder of the beauty and strength that resides in the human spirit."
—Angeles Arrien, cultural anthropologist
and award-winning author

". . . JL Kimmel's dream-like homage to authors Lewis Carroll and Frank Baum. . . . extraordinary paintings . . . enchanting characters and archetypes. . . . Kimmel wants us to believe that there is a more hopeful future for all of humanity. . . ."

—Bob Johnson
Second Saturday Magazine
WPKN/WPKM Radio
Interview Feb. 9, 2008

"(The author) reveals the adventure, tension and magic of the human quest for wholesome maturity. . . . unfolds with an excitement and intensity equaled by its vibrant full-color illustrations. . . . Multi-layered treasures for heart and mind. . . . A not-to-be-missed book!"

—Sister Laura Algiere, DW
Editorial Board of *Wellsprings*, a publication
of the Daughters of Wisdom, U.S. Province

"This magical book is filled with enchantment, exquisite visuals and a compelling story for all ages. You will step into a world of wonder through *The Magic Gown*. Mr. H. Myrrh, a dragon, puts it succinctly, 'Get used to the unusual, kid!' "

—Patrick O'Neill, President
Extraordinary Conversations, Inc.
Author of *The Visionmaker*

"I think it's great for kids because they have a really easy time imagining the scenes in the book. The descriptions are as colorful as the pictures they're based on."

—a mother's comment from "Author   Brings
'Magic' to Oceanic Library," by David Apy
The Two River Times, Aug. 24, 2007

". . . a magical story of transformation and hope . . . a reminder of the strength that lives in the human spirit . . . a book that will open your young reader's imagination and creativity."

—Sara Sgarlat
Today's Parent magazine
June/July 2007

The Magic Gown

Wishing you magical
Adventures!

The Magic Gown

J. L. KIMMEL

SPRING TREE
PRESS

Illustrations Copyright © 2007 by J.L. Kimmel
Book design and production by Rohanidesign.net
Gown cover photo by jeffmartinphoto.com

For information, contact:
SPRING TREE PRESS
P.O. Box 461
Atlantic Highlands, NJ 07716
www.springtreepress.com
1-732-872-8002
If you are unable to order this book from you local bookseller,
you may order directly from the publisher.

Call 1-732-872-8002

ISBN 0-9785007-0-9
Printed in Hong Kong

Second printing © 2008

For Ryan and Zack

CONTENTS

ACKNOWLEDGEMENT

Thank you to my editor, Margaret O'Gorman,
for traveling in the Land of Ten Kings and Roses
with me for over a year and loving it. Thank
you to M Leonard Baker, for his excellent
editing and wonderful enthusiasm.

CHAPTER 1

A New Home

One early summer morning, along the shoreline of a golden-lit beach, a white seagull flew in the direction of a girl pulling her green-painted kayak in the sand. As a sudden breeze blew her long, brown, sun-bleached hair away from her tanned face, she looked up and noticed the bird. It circled once over her head, dropping something from its beak.

The girl quickly put out her left hand and caught the small object falling from the sky. It was a shell. She examined it. On the outer side it was bumpy, shimmering gold and pearled white with purple-colored markings on the top end. The inside was smooth and creamy white, with light and dark purple. Squinting her large, sea-green eyes, she looked up to see the bird heading east out over the glistening water.

"Lilly, come on! I want to make the early ferry," she heard her father call from the driveway.

Lilly put the shell into the pocket of her faded, peach-colored summer dress and dragged the kayak through two grassy sand dunes toward the house. When she got to the car, the engine was already running and her father was waiting, smiling.

"You ready to go, Lil?" he asked.

"No! I don't want to move. I like it here. I don't see why we have to go," she said, as her father lifted the kayak on to the top of the car and tightened the rope around it.

"We've already been over this. I have a new job. We've been on this island for six years."

"That's not long."

"You're eleven now."

"So?"

"It will be good for you, honey."

"No, it won't!"

"You can go to school and have friends."

"I have J," she insisted.

"Is that it?" her mother called to them, coming out of the front door with the last of the boxes. "Andrew, Lilly, is there anything else you need from the house before I lock it up?"

"That's it for me, how about you, Lil?"

Lilly looked through the car window to see the cardboard box resting on the seat. Without answering, she got into the backseat and slammed the door closed.

"Okay, then let's go," her father called.

The weathered station wagon pulled away. Her small face watched the beach house through the rear window for as long as she could see it. Once it had disappeared, Lilly turned and put her arm around the cardboard box as the car headed down the road to the ferry that goes to the North Carolina mainland. There they would get on the ocean highway north and drive up the coastline to a small town in New Jersey.

It was well after dark when they arrived a couple of nights later. Lilly stood in the stone driveway outside the old yellow cottage surrounded by the towering silhouettes of locust trees, cedar and white pines, and

looked up at the star-filled sky and the crescent moon. The scent of dried pine needles perfumed the warm night air. She heard a great horned owl hoo-hooing from the thick woods nearby and what sounded like the chirping of thousands of crickets and locust bugs. From the tidal creek beyond the old ivy covered stonewall, water splashed. In the dark, Lilly could not see that it was the resident muskrat taking her summer midnight swim. She dashed back to the car.

"J! You okay? I heard something out there! What do ya think it is? I don't like it here!" she whispered, kneeling next to the cardboard box and opening the top.

The blue jay squawked, looking up from the box at her. She had found him on the island a year ago, when he was just a baby, and fed him things like chopped-up worms, bugs and nuts. Now, although he lived outside, he was tame and would fly to her.

"Tomorrow morning you'll see this place, and if you don't like it either, we can leave!" The bird fluttered around the box. "Okay. You're so brave, J; you're not afraid of the dark like me, are ya?" She carried the bird in the box to the garage, kissed her finger and touched the bird's head, then shut the top. Spooked again by the dark and the new and different sounds, she quickly flipped the light switch off, closed the garage door and ran for the house.

It was a clear, blue-sky morning when Lilly awoke. Out her window she could look down at Clay Pit Creek or directly out at a tall, straight, blue spruce tree. It was like having a perfect Christmas tree outside the window all year round. Holly trees filled with red berries lined the creek edge. Pairs of red cardinals hopped from branch to branch, making little chipping sounds. On the far side of the creek, acres of cattails waved bright green against the early morning light. Flocks of red-winged black birds perched on the tops of the cattails, swaying back and forth. Farther out, the creek led into the river and from there to the ocean. Lilly went to the garage, brought the box outside and opened the top. The blue jay hopped out fluttering his wings, flew to a nearby holly tree and then off to find something to eat. Lilly thought she'd do the same thing. She made two soft-boiled eggs and toast with cinnamon and honey.

Lilly spent the first half of the day fixing up her bedroom. Around lunchtime, her mother came into her room carrying a package and said it was addressed to her. She had found it on the front porch, she explained. It was a plain, brown, cardboard box with no return address.

Lilly opened the package and took out something hard and rectangular, about the size of a small shoebox. It was wrapped in blue paper. Unwrapping the paper carefully, she uncovered a red wooden box carved with hummingbirds and flowering vines. Lilly ran her fingers over the carvings and then opened the box. Inside, wrapped in yellow paper, were tiny black seeds. A neat, white, note card fluttered to the floor. Lilly picked it up and read it. In simple black writing, Lilly read, "Welcome to your new home."

"Who's it from?" she asked her mother, placing the box on the dresser in front of the mirror.

Her mother stood studying the note card.

"I don't know."

Her mother leaned closer to study the carvings.

"Hmmmm . . . hummingbirds."

Lilly took the oyster shell from her pocket to put into the box.

"What's that?" her mother asked.

"A shell!" Lilly snapped.

"I can see that. May I see it, please?"

"I guess so." Lilly handed the shell to her mother.

Katherine held the shell up and said, "Look how it shimmers; it's some kind of oyster shell."

"I know that. A seagull from home gave it to me."

"Oh, really?" her mother said.

"I'm going to make a necklace out of it and wear it all the time 'cause it's from my real home and it's a lucky shell!"

Lilly took the shell back.

"Look how beautiful it is here, Lil," her mother said, looking out the window. "I bet you can even kayak down that creek. Now come on downstairs for lunch. I made your favorite soup."

"I'm not hungry," she replied.

"Well, why don't you go take your kayak out then? But don't go too far."

"Maybe I'll go all the way home with J!"

"Funny, Lil."

"I don't want to go outside anyway."

"Well, it's a beautiful day," her mother said as she left the room.

"You can't stay cooped up in here all day."

"Yes, I can," said Lilly, "and I will, too; I want to go home."

Lilly shut the door as her mother left the room.

"No one ever listens to me!" she yelled.

She opened the red wooden box and placed the shell in it. She took out the yellow paper and carefully examined the tiny seeds with her delicate fingers.

In the afternoon, Lilly found the sunniest window in the house, the living room window facing to the south. She carefully put some of the seeds in a small pot of moist dirt and covered it with a piece of glass. Everyday she would check the seeds and care for them and see what would grow.

That night, Lilly's parents sat on the back porch while Lilly made her shell necklace in the living room.

Katherine shifted closer and spoke softly, "Andrew, I have no idea where that red wooden box and those seeds came from. And that unsigned note? There was no return address. Don't you think that's strange? Who do you think sent it to her?"

"It does seem a little peculiar, but I'm sure it's nothing. Let's see…who could it be from?" he was thinking.

"Something about it seems so familiar it worries me."

"What worries you?"

"The hummingbirds. I don't know . . . but . . . ." She didn't want to say it.

They sat quiet.

"Hmmm . . . What is it? What's bothering you?" he pressed her.

"Maybe there's more to this," she whispered.

"Like what?" he asked.

"Like what happened to Lilly in Brazil," she said.

Andrew sighed.

She looked around and said, "I know it's been more than six years but it's always on my mind."

"I know it is."

"I'm always wondering what actually happened that time at the waterfall and now this strange box with seeds just as we've moved. It makes me worried all over again."

She looked at Andrew.

"It was a mistake to leave the island and come here."

Andrew put his arm around her. "Why would you say that? We agreed it was time."

"Who sent it to her?" Katherine fretted.

"Whoever sent it to her, it was time to get off that island. Lilly was so isolated there. It will be good for Lilly. It will be good for all of us."

"I hope so."

Andrew Segovia, Lilly's father, was, among many things, a pianist and a composer. Born in Spain, he had moved to Rio de Janeiro, Brazil to work. Lilly's mother, Katherine Kelly Segovia, was a botanical illustrator and had come to Brazil for six months from the United States to illustrate rare orchids in the Brazilian forests for a museum. They met one evening when Katherine was having dinner at a friend's home and Andrew had also been invited. That night they danced and talked late into the night and fell in love. Katherine finished her illustrations but stayed in Brazil. Lilly Segovia soon joined the little family. The family moved from Brazil to North Carolina shortly after a mysterious incident that happened when Lilly was five years old. Like many times before, Katherine had taken Lilly with her into the tropical mountain forest to sketch wild orchids and ferns growing near a fast flowing waterfall. That day Lilly had climbed up alongside the waterfall, where she watched brilliant green and blue hummingbirds around a large vine filled with violet passionflower blossoms. She sat on the rocks watching the hummingbirds play in the delicate shimmering water spray. They hovered around her and the flowers like suspended fluorescent jewels. Lilly smiled and laughed as more and more of the tiny birds surrounded her. Suddenly, her mother could hardly see her. Nervously, Katherine called to Lilly, but the sound of the waterfall and the humming of the birds' wings were too loud. Katherine began to climb toward Lilly, but in her haste she slipped on the rocks. When she regained her footing and looked up, Lilly was gone. Katherine frantically searched around the waterfall. She dove into the deep pool of water below the waterfall and searched the rocky sides. Panicked now, she went to get help. All that day and into the night, Andrew and the police searched for Lilly, but she was nowhere to be found. When they returned home to the house the next morning, they found Lilly in her room asleep in her bed, unharmed. Lilly's parents noticed unusual shimmering silver flecks in her hair, but she remembered only being near the waterfall.

Soon after this incident, Lilly and her parents moved to the beach house Katherine had inherited. Andrew worked on boat engines on the mainland for money and composed music, and Katherine continued her illustration work for books and the museum. For the next six years they lived quietly, simply, and isolated by the ocean. And now they had moved.

During the next few weeks before the school semester started, Lilly climbed the big old trees and kayaked down the creek into the river.

One afternoon she paddled down the river and around the bend while the blue jay sat on the edge of the kayak. As Lilly came around the bend, she saw a woman, a man and a dog standing on the embankment. The dog wagged its tail and barked as she and J went by. The woman and the man looked sad watching her. Lilly waved to them but they stood motionless. As she turned around toward the creek, she wondered about the man and woman and why they looked so sad.

She soon found out from the neighbor, Mrs. London, who lived two houses away. That day Mrs. London had called to her to come visit on her way back up the creek. Lilly had never been to Mrs. London's house before. J and Lilly stopped by just in time for warm

blueberry scones and iced tea with honey. She sat in Mrs. London's kitchen. Lilly told her about seeing the sad man and woman and the dog standing on the river's edge.

"Oh, that's Frank and Mary Finch. Their son, Tom, disappeared not too long ago. He was about your age."

Lilly thought the couple looked old enough to be Tom's grandparents, but she didn't say anything like that.

Mrs. London continued speaking, "It seems he went fishing in his boat one morning just before sunrise and never returned. They sent out a search party but nothing was found, not even his boat."

"Oh, that's terrible. His poor parents must have been so worried and sad. I wonder what happened?"

"They thought maybe he ventured out into the ocean and capsized."

Lilly tried to imagine the boy, thinking how she would have met him when she moved here. "What was he like?"

"Tom used to stop by and visit; he would eat scones and talk to us."

"About what?" Lilly asked, so curious about the missing boy.

"About anything and everything. He loved to talk."

J flew down from a tree limb and landed on the windowsill. Lilly jumped.

"J, you scared me!"

"Who's that?" Mrs. London asked.

"That's J."

"Well, isn't that something," the woman said.

Mrs. London filled a small paper bag with scones.

"Here, Lilly, take these home."

Lilly didn't want to go home; she wanted to know more about Tom, about what he talked about.

"Okay, thank you. I'll come visit again soon."

Paddling home, she was lost in thought thinking about Tom Finch. She wished she had met him.

School soon started and Lilly would catch the bus at the end of the driveway. Sometimes in the morning, as she walked down the long stone driveway, deer would be eating the apples and pears on the ground from the fruit trees in the front yard. The trees began to change to reds and yellows. In the living room window, a small leafy plant grew in the pot.

CHAPTER 2

A Visit

On Halloween Lilly dressed in a costume she had made herself. She made wings out of crimson-red silk and wire, with shimmering sheer pink and gold trim, and she wore fresh pink lilies and red roses around her neck and in her hair. She wandered down different streets collecting candy with some new friends from school. On her way home she saw a house with a glowing pumpkin face on the porch, so she thought she would make one more stop to collect a little more candy. It was the last house on the street. As she approached the porch steps, she noticed the cut-out pumpkin face looked sad. Walking up the porch, she heard a dog barking. The door swung open before Lilly could knock. Standing in the doorway was a woman with a large bowl in her hand. Lilly recognized the woman from the river embankment. It was Mary Finch, Tom's mother.

"Well, look what we have here," called out the woman warmly. "You are the first little red angel we've had all night!"

Lilly giggled nervously. "Hello. Uh . . . trick or treat."

The woman held out the bowl of candy. Lilly took a chocolate candy bar from the bowl and put it in her candy bag.

"Thank you," said Lilly and went to turn away. "Oh, please take another one," the woman insisted. "That's a beautiful costume! Isn't it, dear?" The woman was talking to a man who came into the entrance hallway and out onto the porch.

"Yes, it is," he responded. It was Mr. Finch.

"Thank you. I'm a red fairy bird," Lilly said shyly.

Just then a big yellow furry dog came bouncing out of the house toward Lilly.

Lilly bent down to greet him. "Hi, there!" she exclaimed. The dog was now on its back, wiggling and wagging his tail, happy for her attention.

"That's Jake, Tom's dog," the man commented. "I see he really likes the red fairy bird." He laughed.

Lilly giggled again and kept petting Jake, not knowing what to say next.

Mr. Finch looked at Mrs. Finch and said, "Hey, she's the girl who goes by in the green kayak with the bird. Aren't you?" he asked Lilly.

Lilly stood up, answering, "Yes, I am, and the bird is J. He's my pet blue jay. I brought him here when we moved."

"Very interesting. Well, I am Frank Finch," he said heartily, extending his right hand to her.

"And I'm Mary Finch; it's so nice to meet you. And what is your name?" asked Mrs. Finch, as she touched Lilly's red silk wing.

"Lilly Segovia. I live down on Clay Pit Creek in the yellow house before the old cemetery. I moved there in August," she replied.

"You sound like you came from the south or somethin'," Frank Finch said.

"Yes, North Carolina, and before that I lived in Brazil," she replied.

"Very interesting," he repeated.

"I wish you could have met our son, Tom; I think you are probably about the same age, twelve or so," Mrs. Finch said.

"I'll be twelve in May," Lilly answered, then hesitated. "I'm sorry about your son; Mrs. London told me what happened."

"Thank you, dear. Would you like to see a picture of him?"

Before Lilly could answer, Mary Finch stepped into the foyer, took a framed photograph from the table and came out to the porch.

Lilly held the picture under the porch light. She looked at the dark haired boy next to the boat. For a moment, time seemed to stand still.

"That's Tom and his boat," said Mr. Finch, breaking the silence.

"Oh, he looks very nice," said Lilly, still looking at the picture.

"Yes, he was. I mean, is," Mrs. Finch said, getting flustered. Mr. Finch put his arm around her.

Lilly looked up, "Oh . . . I'm sorry." She gave the picture back to Mrs. Finch. "Umm . . . well, I better be getting home now. It's really dark. Thank you for the candy." She turned, rushing down the steps.

"Please come visit us again, little red angel! I mean, fairy bird," Mary Finch said.

"Bye, Lilly, nice to meet ya," called Frank Finch.

"Okay, I will. Bye," Lilly called back. "Bye, Jake," she shouted, as she ran down the street. Her red silk wings were bouncing in the autumn night, and she wished J would find her to keep her company in the dark!

The next morning, Lilly hurried downstairs to have breakfast. As she passed through the living room, she smelled a light sweet fragrance.

"Wow!" she called out.

On the windowsill, the plant had grown. It had suddenly bloomed with four different colored blossoms. There was a rosy-pink flower, a buttery yellow one, a violet purple and a cinnamon orange. She called her mother and father to come see them.

"They look like some kind of rose blossom to me, but none I've ever seen before," Katherine commented, as the three of them stood staring in astonishment at the exquisite fragrant flowers. That afternoon, Lilly

was playing in the woods when her father called to her. She appeared at the edge of the woods and saw her parents standing in the driveway.

"We're going out to do some errands," her father said.

"Will you give the soup on the stove a stir, Lil? I put it on low," her mother asked. She had made a pot of Lilly's favorite: creamy curry noodle soup.

"Sure," Lilly responded.

"We'll be back soon, Lil," said her father.

"Okay, bye." Lilly watched them pull down the long driveway and went back into the woods. J hopped from branch to branch above her, listening to her sing as she collected pinecones in a basket.

"Get along, little doggie, get along, get along.
Move along, little darlin', move along, move along.
Little baby, do you love me?
You know I love you.
Can you feel my heart beating?
I feel yours too.
It's true the night is falling, when angels stroke your head.
In the daylight, your momma's calling, move along, move along."

In a little while, Lilly came back into the house carrying the basket full of pinecones. She could smell the soup cooking and hurried to the kitchen to stir it. As she came into the kitchen, she heard loud bubbling noises and saw the lid of the large cooking pot moving and jumping on the stovetop. Soup spurted out. Moving closer, Lilly noticed the flame wasn't even on.

That's funny, she thought, when suddenly the lid lifted completely off the pot. "Ahhh!" Lilly jumped back. Just then, a bright blue swan flew out of the pot and settled on the kitchen table with a ruffle of its feathers and a flap of its wings.

Lilly dropped the basket of pinecones and covered her eyes. She stood frozen in place. The pinecones were sprawled across the kitchen floor around her feet.

"Hello, Lilly dear," the bird said in a woman's voice. "Get some soup and sit with me."

With her eyes still covered, Lilly stood silent for a few seconds. She tried to speak but could only manage, in a whisper, to utter, "No, go away!"

"Go away? Come sit with me, please. I won't hurt you. I have a message for you."

Lilly wanted to hide somewhere until the bird went away, but somehow she couldn't leave.

Lilly moved her fingers slightly away from her eyes and said, "You're still here."

"Of course I am. Come sit with me."

"No . . . I can't."

"Yes, you can. Of course you can," encouraged the swan. "But first get some soup."

Lilly took a deep breath, slowly stepped over the pinecones, moved toward the cabinet and reached for a bowl. Her hands were shaking. She spilled the soup as she tried to fill the bowl.

"You'll feel better after you have some of that delicious soup your mother made. I see you're wearing the Shell of Great Fortune and Mysterious Ways," the swan commented.

Lilly touched the shell around her neck. "I am? It's just an oyster shell."

She walked toward the swan. "Mysterious Ways? What's that mean? That sounds terrible." Lilly looked pale as she came nearer the table.

"Sit, dear. No, not terrible. Wonderful! Now taste the soup and you'll feel better. It's your favorite, isn't it?"

Lilly sat in the chair. "Yes. How do you know that?" Lilly tasted a spoonful of the warm spicy soup. She peeked up at the swan sitting serenely on her kitchen table watching her.

"I know a lot about you, a very lot," the swan replied.

"Why? . . . But who are you?"

"How rude of me," said the swan. "I never introduced myself. I am Zara Bluewood, from the Blue Tree Forest."

"Oh," said Lilly, scrunching her face. She ate more soup.

The swan continued: "Just after sunrise, around the time of the crescent moon, the shell was returned to you. Then the red box came with the seeds, and you planted them just like you were supposed to. Today the rose blossoms summoned me."

"Oh," repeated Lilly, even more bewildered, almost dizzy.

"How do you like your new home, dear?"

"It's good. I like it. Where's the Blue Tree Forest? Brazil?"

"No, not Brazil," chuckled Zara Bluewood.

Then, stretching her long lovely blue neck, the swan leaned toward Lilly.

Her black beak nearly touched Lilly's nose, and her black eyes stared right through to Lilly's soul. "Lilly?"

"Yes?" whispered Lilly.

"I have come to tell you that magic is swirling all around, waiting, waiting, waiting."

Lilly inhaled, her eyes wide. "Waiting for what?"

"When the time is right and the night is white, you will visit us," Zara Bluewood answered.

"Visit where?" asked Lilly.

"Where your shell came from," said Zara.

"North Carolina?" said Lilly, holding the shell with both her hands.

Lilly broke the swan's gaze and looked down into her soup bowl. "I couldn't possibly go anywhere like that . . . This can't be happening."

"Of course it is happening. Don't be afraid," said the swan. "The time has come."

Lilly looked up. The table was empty.

Lilly suddenly heard a clatter of wings outside the kitchen window.

"Aaaagh!" she screamed and jumped up from the table, knocking over the bowl. She ran through the pinecones, out of the room and out the back door to her kayak. As she paddled up the river, J joined her, sitting on the edge. "J, I must be seeing things. How is it possible that a blue swan named Zara Bluewood from the Blue Tree Forest flew out of our soup pot? She said that magic is all around and that I am wearing the Shell of Great Fortune and Mysterious something. Tell me, J, am I going crazy or what?"

J squawked back at her.

Lilly stopped paddling and sat quietly in the kayak in the middle of the river. "What am I gonna do now?" she asked herself. "I'm just not gonna think about it, that's all!"

After a while, she turned around and paddled home.

"Lilly, what happened in here?" her mother asked, looking down at the basket of spilled pinecones on the kitchen floor, the knocked-over bowl and the puddles of soup on the stovetop.

Already she was reminded of the incredible blue swan incident: *How could I possibly say to my mother, "Oh yeah, a blue swan named Zara Bluewood from the Blue Tree Forest flew out of the soup and said, 'Hello, Lilly, magic is all around,' which scared me to death and I dropped the pinecones on the floor and spilled the soup and I ate soup with her and when the blue swan disappeared from the table I ran out of the house." No way can I say that!*

"Sorry, Mom . . . Um . . . That crazy bird scared me. I'll clean it up."

"J?" her mother asked, puzzled. She picked up the bowl, shaking her head from side to side. "Well anyway, how was the soup?"

"Oh yeah, it was good." Lilly collected the pinecones on the floor, trying to stay away from the soup pot.

I'm just not gonna think about it, she thought.

CHAPTER 3

When The Night Is White

Christmas day dawned very cold and clear. For a Christmas gift,
Lilly's mother had given her a handmade book of painted lilies of
all kinds, the flower she was named after.

In the afternoon, Lilly took a walk to Mary and Frank Finch's house. She carried with her a clay pot with a small rose plant she had started from the mysterious seeds. As she walked up the steps, Jake began to bark. Mary Finch arrived at the door without her knocking.

"Well, look who is visiting us on Christmas, Frank," she said, calling to him in the other room. "It's the little red angel."

J had followed Lilly and he now landed on the porch railing. Jake barked and ran over to the blue jay, but the bird stood its ground, squawking comically at the dog.

"That's quite a bird you have there," Frank Finch said, walking out onto the porch and giving her a hug. "Merry Christmas, Lilly. It's so nice of you to visit us today. Please come in for a little while." He held the door open so she could walk under his arm into the hall, passing Tom's picture sitting on the hall table.

"Mrs. Finch, do you have a sunny window for this rose bush I started for you? You can plant it in the ground in the spring," Lilly said, handing the pot to her.

Mary took the pot from Lilly.

"Oh, thank you, honey. I have the perfect spot; the window that looks out to the river is sunny all afternoon. What kind of rose bush is this?" Mrs. Finch asked. "I can't wait to see the blossoms."

"They're special roses," replied Lilly.

"Well, they're certainly special, because they're from you," said Mrs. Finch.

Mrs. Finch and Lilly walked into the room that faced the river. She put the pot down on the table beside a few scraggly geranium plants.

"These geraniums need to be cut back and fed," said Lilly.

"Oh, would you do it for me while you're here?" asked Mary Finch. "I'll get the plant food and cutters."

"Okay."

Lilly walked into the foyer and picked up the picture of Tom, studying every detail of his face.

Putting the picture down, she went back into the room and sat in a big chair that looked out of the picture window facing the river. The river was still and the edges were full of ice.

I bet Tom liked to sit in this chair and watch the river, she thought.

Mrs. Finch came into the room with the plant food, water and the cutting shears.

"You know a lot about flowers, don't you, dear?"

"I love flowers. My mother draws them for books. I'm named after a flower, the stargazer lily."

"Oh, how lovely," Mrs. Finch responded. Then she paused for a moment, lost in her thoughts. "That was the name of Tom's boat . . . is the name. Oh, dear."

"What is?" Lilly asked.

"Star-Gazer," answered Mary, composing herself.

Lilly blushed and began to trim the geraniums. "Wow."

She gave the rose bush a little water and fed the geraniums.

"Take a look at the ornament on the top of the tree, Lilly," said Mary, pointing to the corner.

In the corner of the room was a small decorated Christmas tree. One ornament, hanging near the top, was a miniature carved wooden boat with the name Star-Gazer painted on the side.

"Tom made it last year out of some driftwood. It's a replica of his boat."

Lilly was quiet, studying the wooden boat.

Mary sat down in the big chair and sighed.

"This was Tom's favorite place to sit and watch the river and look at his books. Ever since he came to us, he has been so special."

"What do you mean?"

"You see, Tom was adopted by Frank and me when he was a baby."

Lilly sat in front of her on the floor.

"It's hard to believe it's been almost twelve years since Frank and I went to visit his sister, who lives up north in Whitehorse, Canada. She worked in an orphanage there, and she told us about a baby that was brought to them in the spring by a mountain man who had found the baby boy far in the mountains by Mt. Logan. The mountain man took care of him until he could travel out of the high country. The mountain man could never be found after that. We adopted the miracle mountain baby."

"Wow, that's amazing," said Lilly.

"Yes, it is. I miss our special boy so much."

Mary leaned from the chair and stroked Lilly's cheek.

"Thank you so much for visiting us today and bringing the rose bush. You cheered me up."

"You're welcome." Lilly wanted to ask a million more questions about Tom but didn't. "I'll come back soon and see how all the plants are doing, if that's okay?"

"Oh, Frank and I would love that, wouldn't we, Frank?"

Mr. Finch had come walking into the room. "That would be great."

Out the picture window, the sun was low in the winter sky.

"I better go home now."
"Come back soon," called Frank Finch.
"Bye, Lil; thank you!" called Mary.
"Bye."

The day after Christmas the clouds moved in, and by the afternoon it had begun to snow. By nighttime the snow was really coming down. The fire crackled and flickered in the fireplace in the living room, where her father played Chopin on the piano. The music floated upstairs, where Lilly sat in the comfy corner chair wrapped in a blanket in her bedroom, looking at the hand made flower book her mother gave her. When her eyes grew heavy, she climbed into bed and drifted away to sleep.

All was silent except for the sound of the trickling creek water of the incoming tide and the flapping of wings echoing down the creek from the river. A big white seagull flew through the snow toward Lilly's house. As the bird flew past her bedroom window, the tip of its wing touched the glass, making a soft brushing sound. The flower book fell from the chair onto the floor. Startled, Lilly woke up and looked around the room.

"Oh, no!"

Her bedroom door was now a bright-colored blue. It had pink flowers like lilacs growing around it. A soft yellow-green glow filled the room from outside the door.

"Mommy, Daddy!" she yelled.

No one answered her.

"Mommy, Daddy! Answer me!"

She ran to the window and saw that it was snowing so hard she couldn't see out.

She sat in the chair, pulled the blanket around her and looked at the blue door.

Blue door, she thought.

"It's blue!" she said out loud.

"And the night's white . . . and . . . oh, no!" she said. "Zara Bluewood!"

"Zara?" she called out. "Are you there? Is this the magic?"

Lilly heard Zara's voice coming from the blue door.

"The time has come so long forbidden, until now this magic hidden.

Wonderful, wonderful," whispered her voice. "O sweet child, let us rejoice.

Another door has opened!"

"Zara?" Lilly called out. She stood up, wrapped in the blanket, and tiptoed toward the door. Looking through, she called her again, "Zara?"

Through the door there was a strange little room with pale-green misty walls and a red and white checkered floor like a chessboard.

"Zara," she called again. "Answer me. Is this the magic? I don't like it. You are scaring me."

Barefooted, Lilly stepped onto the red and white floor. She could hear ocean sounds. The green misty walls slowly became transparent and completely disappeared. Lilly now found herself standing at the water's edge of an unfamiliar beach of peach-colored sand. Out over the turquoise water, something was flying toward her. As it got closer, she saw that it was a white seagull with something in its beak. The bird landed at the water's edge near her bare feet. In its beak was an iridescent orange and gold fish. The fish wriggled and began to speak. It had a much deeper voice than you would think it could have.

"Hello, Lilly. The first snowfall is magical, as you can see.

"I am The Fish, a messenger, and this is Tu, your dream guardian."

Tu bowed to her as The Fish wiggled in his beak.

"Where am I? Where's Zara?"

She couldn't believe she was talking to a fish in a bird's mouth.

"You are in the Peach Sand Cove in the Land of Ten Kings and Roses."

Lilly touched the oyster shell necklace.

"Did you give me this? Was that you?" she asked Tu.

Tu nodded his head yes.

"Tu brought it to you this time."

"What do you mean, this time?"

"Remember the waterfall, where Princess Anais first gave you the Shell of Great Fortune and Mysterious Ways?" The Fish asked.

"No."

"When your mother took you to the waterfall in the forest?" The Fish replied.

"I remember lots of hummingbirds around me by a waterfall and then the waterfall . . . ." Lilly suddenly stopped.

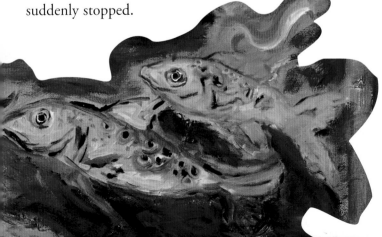

"Don't be afraid. Princess Anais of Beetle Island gave you that shell and she wears the other half," The Fish went on. "At the waterfall you dropped the shell into the pool below. You dove in after it but became very frightened, and Tu found you under the water and returned you to your home.

Lilly looked at him. "Thank you, Tu."

The bird bowed.

"Who gave me the shell?"

"Princess Anais; she is coming here to meet you. She has something for you. She was supposed to be here already," The Fish declared.

"Where is she? What is it?" Lilly asked, excited and nervous at the same time to meet a Princess who wears the same shell necklace as hers.

Suddenly a large wave came in, and the water pulled at her legs so strong it knocked her over onto the sand. Tu flew from the sand. Lilly began to feel very lightheaded and heard the sound of Tu's flapping wings getting louder and closer. He flew close to her face and The Fish kissed her on the forehead. Very dizzy, Lilly closed her eyes to steady herself.

"The tide is going out. Princess Anais has not come. We must go. You must leave now . . . we'll meet again."

Lilly drifted and was soon asleep. She awoke much later than usual the next morning. It was still snowing.

CHAPTER 4

Down in the Cellar

"Looks like we're in for a lot more snow," her father called, as Lilly hurried down the stairs, leaping from the third step and jumping into him as he came around the corner.

"Hey! Where're you flying to today, little bird?"

She giggled.

"Hi, Daddy."

"Mornin', Lil," her mother said to her from the kitchen. "You feeling okay?"

Lilly stood in the doorway. "Yeah, fine. Why?" Lilly scrunched her face up.

"What's that face about? You slept so late, that's all. It's noon."

"Wow, it is?" Lilly shrugged.

"You want some pancakes?"

"Yes, please, with maple syrup and bananas!"

Katherine poured the batter onto the griddle. Lilly sat down at the table just as J landed on the snow-covered windowsill outside.

"J!"

"Okay, okay, I'll be out soon!" Lilly said through the glass.

"Squawk!" he replied. Then, tap-tap-tap, he pecked on the glass. "Squawk! Squawk!"

"He said 'Okay, and don't forget a pancake,'" she told her mother.

"Lil speaks blue jay; imagine that!" her mother laughed, flipping the hot cakes.

Later in the afternoon, smoke rose from the chimney of the yellow house as the fire crackled inside and the snow fell down heavy outside.

The front door whipped open and Lilly came back into the house covered in snow. Snow blew into the entrance behind her. The wind was howling now, and you couldn't see anything in the blowing snow. It was a blizzard for sure.

Her mother met her. "Lil, where have you been? I was so worried about you out there in this."

"With J, playing. I built a snow cave for him under the big white pine."

"You should have told me you were going outside. Don't forget to knock the snow off your boots and shake your coat outside," her mother said, walking back into the kitchen.

"I have some nice hot soup, your favorite, creamy curry noodle."

Lilly approached the steaming soup pot. She lifted the lid and peeked carefully into the pot.

"What are ya looking for, Lil?"

"Nothing."

"My paints and brushes are all set up in my studio downstairs if you want to paint, Lil."

"Okay, thanks."

After her second bowl, Lilly walked to the cellar door and opened it slowly. Looking down the steps, she carefully descended them. She stood at the easel, painting a snow scene of two deer standing in a pine tree forest. Shwoooooo, the wind howled, as the blowing snow piled up against the basement window. Shwoooooo, rattle, rattle.

"More dark green," Lilly said to herself and reached for the tube of green paint.

"Purrrrrrrrrrrrrr, purrrrrrrrr," she heard, then little panting breaths, then, "purrrrrrrrrr, purrrrrrrrrrrrr."

Sounds like a cat, she thought, *but we don't have a cat!*

It was coming from behind her.

Lilly turned slowly from the easel, holding the tube of green paint.

"Uhhhhh!" she gasped. Paint squirted from the tube into the air.

Two cat people stood looking at her. Lilly wanted to bolt, to run up the stairs, but the cat people stood in her way. One cat person was tall and wore an orange, gold and red-feathered headdress, like a crown. The other one was very short, with a smaller feathered crown. It had green paint on its face. Lilly's heart pounded so loud she could hear it.

She moved backwards, knocking over the paint tubes and brushes. The tall one, who had bright yellow-green cat eyes, suddenly spoke.

"Shhhh," the big cat creature said.

"Who are you?" Lilly blurted out.

It spoke quietly, almost like a purr with words.

"I'm King Rue and this is Mik. We are from the Red Tree Forest in the Land of Ten Kings and Roses, where the red wooden box is from."

He had an unusual accent, like someone from ancient Egypt or somewhere.

The dream of the blue door, The Fish and Tu flooded back into her memory.

"Oh, no! Do you want the box back now?" asked Lilly. "I'll go get it."

She hurried to go around him to the stairs, but the cat man gently blocked her way.

"No need for that, Lilly. It was a gift."

They heard footsteps at the top of the stairs.

"Lilly, are you all right?" Lilly's mother suddenly called down the stairs.

Rue put his long cat finger over Lilly's lips and nodded his head yes.

Lilly, barely catching her breath, answered, "Uh . . . yeah. Uh . . . I just knocked over the brushes."

"Be careful with that stuff, okay, Lil?"

"Okay."

They heard her mother's footsteps move away from the basement door.

"What about Zara the swan, The Fish and Tu? Where are they? This is crazy! I'm going crazy, aren't I? Do I have a fever? I must be delirious." Lilly felt her forehead.

"No, no, no, quite the contrary," said the tall cat man. "You don't have a fever and you are not delirious. You are clear as a crystal bell."

Mik made grunting purring sounds, nodding his head in agreement as he fiddled with a gold rock about the size of a lemon. His lemon yellow eyes stared at Lilly. He smiled. Lilly suddenly noticed he had little pointy teeth, like a cat.

"Oh," she moaned, "I don't feel so good."

She held her stomach.

Rue laughed and said, "Oh, don't mind him; he's not used to seeing someone from your world, but he insisted on coming along with me. He can be very stubborn and persistent, but actually he has been very good company so far."

Again, Mik smiled, grunted and purred, as if he was pleased to hear that he had been good company. He began to pick up the brushes and hand them to Lilly.

"Helpful, too," Rue laughed.

Hesitantly, she took them.

"Thank you, Mik."

"Grunt, grunt," responded Mik.

Lilly turned with the brushes in her hand and saw that the basement stairs were no longer the plain old gray-painted wooden steps. They now glowed yellow and orange. The door was glowing too. It was no longer the plain basement door. Instead, it was arched and beautifully carved, similar to the red box. "Last night, Princess Anais was to visit you at the Peach Sand Cove with something special, but . . ." Rue started to say.

Lilly interrupted him.

"That's it. I'm outta here!" she said, and tried to push past them but couldn't.

"Let me go by!" she demanded.

"Princess Anais was on her way to you, but her ship was attacked. She has been taken by the horrible Lacks, by Moregrott. He wants it."

"Wants what?"

"The Magic Gown, the ancient magic dress."

"We have been sent here to tell you this. You need to go back there now."

Lilly went pale.

"Where? To the Land of Ten Kings and Roses?"

"Yes," Rue answered.

Mik patted her on the arm and she pulled away.

"No! How? Why me?"

"It is not for me to say," Rue answered, as he pointed to the stairs.

Little Mik grunted and nudged Lilly toward the stairs.

Pulling away, she insisted, "I couldn't possibly go. Where's Zara? Is she doing this? Besides, look at the weather; there's a blizzard outside."

The wind howled and the basement window shuddered.

"That's not a problem where you are going. The time has come," he assured her.

"I don't like the way that sounds. No, I can't go! My parents will worry about me. My mother worries about me all the time as it is. She is already a nervous person and even worse since the red box came. They will call the police if I disappear. Here, take the shell back!" she insisted, starting to take the necklace off.

"The shell can never be given back."

"But I don't want it."

"That's not true or you would never have been given it," Rue said. "The second door awaits you now, Lilly. Time moves differently where you are going and you must go now."

"You're scaring me. Go away." Lilly sat down on the bottom step.

Rue's big paw took her hand and she reluctantly stood up. Mik took her other hand. They helped her to the second step. She heard

Rue speaking a strange language. Mik nudged her up the stairs.

"This can't be happening. Someone help me," she whispered.

"Help is on the way. They will help you, Lilly, but you must meet them first," said Rue.

The door blew opened. She saw a black onyx and white pearl-checkered floor that went on into the distance and a vast blue sky.

She looked down at Rue and Mik.

"Who will help me?"

"Turn around. Don't look at us. Listen to my words."

As Rue spoke, colors of all kinds—red, yellow, green and orange—began to swirl around her. They pulled at her like windy hands. She shut her eyes. It was a blowing hurricane of color. She could no longer hear Rue. She felt herself being pulled by the colorful winds.

When she opened her eyes, she was standing on a floor that was moving. It was a red, yellow, orange and green floor. She saw two see-through people of vivid colors with flowing wings sitting at a bright blue table. They greeted her in their language that sounded like the wind moving through the leaves, or like the wind on a mountaintop, or the sound the wind makes moving over the surface of the ocean.

"Hello. Are you wind angels?" asked Lilly.

One, with short moving-air hair, spoke. Lilly's hair blew back with his wind breath.

"I am King of the Colorful Wind."

"And I am Queen of the Colorful Wind."

"I'm Lilly," she said, as she walked a little closer to them.

"We know. Come here, little one. Sit down with us."

The Wind King summoned her.

Lilly crossed the colorful moving floor and sat down at the blue table.

"Are you afraid of us?" asked the Wind Queen.

"No, I love the wind," responded Lilly.

"Very good. We are pleased to hear that, Lilly," the Queen said.

Lilly looked around at the swirling colors.

"Where is this?"

"You are in the center of the Realm of the Colorful Wind, the place of endings and true beginnings. It is where the Magic Gown came from long ago, before it came to the Land of Ten Kings and Roses."

Just then, out from a swirl of red color, a rosy red butterfly flew within inches of Lilly's face.

"Hi," it said, then kissed her on the tip of her nose and fluttered away.

Lilly giggled. "Hello."

"That was Theresa," the Queen told her. "She appears whenever change is in the air."

"Or when you are about to enter the Great Desert of Uncertainty," added the Wind King.

Lilly stopped giggling. "Where?"

The Queen blew a gentle breeze. Lilly took a breath and inhaled the sweet comforting fragrance of the special roses. The Wind King and Queen began to speak again in the strange wind language and pointed to the shell around Lilly's neck. Lilly clasped the shell and listened, mesmerized by their voices. Shimmering colors of gold, silver and green swirled from their hands and touched the shell necklace. The colorful wind blew stronger and Lilly's hair flew back.

Bright colors moved around them, and the wind angels blended into the air and disappeared. Lilly was spinning in a spiral of gold, silver and green. It was the end of something and the beginning too.

CHAPTER **5**

Mr. H. Myrrh

The wind finally stopped and so did the spinning. Lilly now found herself standing at the bottom of three golden steps. Two purple, blue and green palm trees, with purple coconuts, stood on either side of two open, dark, purple-blue doors. Two crossed, light-blue-colored swords were carved on the doors. Through the doors she could see the night sky and a crescent moon shining over an endless desert. Behind her was an impenetrable wall of colorful moving wind from which she could faintly hear the voices of the Wind King and Wind Queen.

She walked up the stairs and stood in front of the open doors, leaning forward a little to peek through. She saw a flat desert that went on and on.

"Wind Angels . . . I want to go home now!" she called out.

She looked around. Nothing happened, nothing changed.

"This could be a dream."

She leaned through the opening of the doors again and put one foot onto the sand, then took it back.

"There's no Magic Gown! This is ridiculous!"

She listened, as if she expected someone to disagree with her. She tried the other foot and took it back too.

"I wish J were here."

Clutching the shell around her neck, she stepped through the doors onto the sand but stopped dead in her tracks.

"Now what? I can't move. I can't move."

She thought about horrible Lacks and other dangers.

"Maybe they know I'm here," she whispered.

Scaring herself, Lilly ran across the barren sand toward the crescent moon suspended in the black starless sky.

There was nothing but flat sand as far as she could see. But soon she began noticing little lumps of something up ahead. Reaching for a lump, she saw that it was a gold rock just like the one Mik had had down in the cellar. Then she saw another one and another one and more and more. At first, she picked up the nuggets as she came across them, like pretty stones on a beach, but soon they got so heavy she couldn't carry them anymore. So she put them down on the sand, spelling her name out like she did at the shore sometimes with seashells. Lilly continued to walk, following the gold rocks.

Maybe this is a trail, she wondered.

What am I talking about?

Then she stopped and yelled, as if someone were listening.

"I can be stubborn and persistent just like little Mik, you know!" Picking up one of the gold rocks, she threw it at the dark, starless sky.

"I like stars. Where are they? Why kind of place doesn't have stars? A dumb place, that's what kind."

Wondering about the stars made her forget she was afraid for a little while.

She sighed. Again she talked to herself, finding comfort in her own voice.

"What a mess I've gotten myself into! What are Mommy and Daddy gonna think, that I just disappeared? Again?"

Lilly thought she saw a shadow or something pass in front of the crescent moon. She looked and saw it again. It seemed to be coming toward her. It was big. It was huge. It was an enormous winged dragon.

Lilly ran as fast as she could. Looking back at the dragon, she didn't see a pile of skeleton bones and tripped over them. She stumbled hard and fell near the edge of a huge crack in the desert floor. The sand fell around her as she went sliding over the edge. Lilly grabbed at the sand and caught the foot of a skeleton leg sticking out of the desert.

Lilly hung swaying in the crack. Suddenly the ground shook as the dragon landed. It placed its large feet, as big as cars, with long red toenails, on the sand. Lilly hung perfectly still, pressed against the wall, clutching onto the bony foot. Snap! The big toe from the foot broke off. Lilly held on tighter. She gasped as the dragon bent over the edge of the crack and looked right at her, with wild green eyes and gold liquid dripping from its mouth.

"I do not think it's your destiny to fall into the Crack of Despair," it said, as it reached toward her with its long claws.

The dragon pulled her up just as the entire foot broke from the ankle and fell into the bottomless crack. The dragon picked up the rest of the skeletons and bones.

"I like to keep the place as neat as possible," he said.

He threw the bones down the crack and they both bent over to watch them fall.

"You don't want to go down there, kid! That's a one-way trip to the City of Grott. Not good, not good!"

Then the dragon stood up straight. He was as tall as the tallest building Lilly had ever been in. She had to crane her neck to see him. As the dragon spoke, big splashes of gold liquid spit out of its mouth and hardened into gold rocks when they hit the ground.

"So you must be Lilly; I saw your name written on the sand with the gold rocks."

"Yes, that's me," she said, trembling.

"Well, I guess you're not here for the gold, are you?" the dragon declared. "Because if you were, you'd be dead by now, like all the others that have come to the Great Desert of Uncertainty looking only for dragon's gold!"

"Oh no, I'm not looking for gold. I'm looking for Princess Anais."

"You're not a Lack, are you?" she asked.

"No, I'm surely not!" he snapped.

"Well, I've never seen one before. Sorry!"

"O hideous putrid things. Their odor could even knock a flying desert dragon over," he told her.

"A flying desert dragon, is that what you are?"

"Yes, that's right. The Lacks, they try to trick me but nothing can hide their vile stench. I haven't seen or smelled a Lack around here for a few days. Every once in a while, I see one peak out of the Well of Unfathomable Suffering or the Crack of Despair to see if I'm close by. It seems they're afraid of me, and with good reason," he boasted, as his eyes looked wild and his tail began to pound the ground.

"Mr. H. Myrrh is my name, by the way, a dragon king."

"Wow, a dragon king! And what's that you say about a well?"

"Yes, the Well of Unfathomable Suffering! And the nastiest bunch of Lacks slithered out of it and into the Silver Sea not too long ago. It was Moregrott. He's the meanest of all Lacks."

The dragon wrinkled his face in disgust.

"Mr. H. Myrrh, this Moregrott has taken Princess Anais. She has something they want very badly . . ."

She stopped speaking, wondering if she should have said that or dare mention the Magic Gown. Maybe he was not to be trusted either. The ground shook as the dragon sat down, shaking his head side to side, disturbed by the news.

"It was Moregrott then! If he has taken Princess Anais, he is after the Magic Gown."

So he does know about the Magic Gown, Lilly thought.

"What do you know?" she asked.

"The gown has been in this land for a long, long time bringing wonderful magic.

"Moregrott knows nothing of wonderful magic and would destroy precious land and hurt anyone who gets in the way of what he wants. He only knows power and greed!"

"Oh, no," said Lilly, and sat down next to him.

"I'm looking for her, see," Lilly said, showing him the shell necklace.

"So you're the girl from the other world who wears the shell!" He stood up. "Well, well, we better get you going on your way. One Well of Unfathomable Suffering coming up!"

"What? No! No way!" exclaimed Lilly. "I'm not going down that, Mr. Myrrh."

"What did you call me?"

"Sorry, I mean Mr. H. Myrrh."

"Thank you."

Mr. H. Myrrh began to walk toward the crescent moon. Lilly ran to keep up with him.

"Isn't there any other way to get out of here and find the Princess and the Magic Gown?

"I really don't want to go down that well. I'm afraid of the dark."

"No, I'm afraid not."

The desert shook with each step he took.

As they went along, she explained to him how the shell fell from the bird's mouth the morning she was moving and how Zara had flown out of the creamy curry noodle soup and told her that magic was all around her and about the riddle, "when the time is right and the night is white."

"Oh, that was an easy one, Lilly," Mr. H. Myrrh commented.

"Yeah, I suppose it was," she replied, "but I didn't expect to visit a talking fish and Tu, my dream guardian, on a peach-colored sand cove or to have cat people visiting with me down in my basement or to meet the King and Queen of the Colorful Wind, and now you and this horrible Well of Unfathomammal Suff . . ."

"Unfathomable Suffering, Lilly. Well, that's what happens when magic is all around you. Get used to the unusual, kid," he laughed.

The dragon explained to Lilly about the Lacks, who climbed up the Well to the desert.

"At first they weren't so bad, even though they weren't easy to look at or be around: they were just hideous creatures," he told her. "Then the greedier they got, the worse they smelled. It became unbearable!"

He told her about those who came into the desert only for the dragon's gold. "Taking dragon's gold is fatal. It must be given." The dragon would find them dead, and he would take their hair and throw their skeletons down into the Well or into the Crack of Despair.

"Wow," said Lilly, "horrible, smelly, Lack creatures climbing out of the Well and you throwing corpses into it, and now you expect me to climb down it! I don't think so."

"No, you don't have to climb down, my dear, that's what the hair rope is for," he assured her.

"Gross," said Lilly.

Lilly began to tire from trying to keep up with the dragon's big footsteps, so he scooped her up, placed her on his back between his purple wings, and flew up into the night sky.

"Mr. H. Myrrh, where are all the stars?" she asked.

"What are you talking about? Can't you see them? They're all around us, the sky is filled with stars," he yelled back to her as he flew toward the crescent moon.

But Lilly couldn't see them. She felt sad about that but maybe he was tricking her. He seemed like a real prankster. She thought he was joking about the dead bodies and the hair rope until she began to see down below dead bodies with big piles of gold rocks near them.

"I'll have to tidy up later," said the dragon, "and throw those gold robber corpses down the Well or the Crack. If I don't, tiny wiggling things like maggots come out of the decaying bones. They are so small you can hardly see them. Then they crawl underneath the desert, way, way down to the dismal City of Grott and grow to become Lacks. It appears there are way more of them then I imagined."

Down below them, Lilly could see what looked like a well. It glowed like the fire in her fireplace at home, and when they landed, Lilly saw that it was lined with dragon's gold which reflected and magnified the crescent moonlight. Next to the Well, she saw a long rope, neatly coiled in a pile. This was the rope made from the hair of the people he found dead. The rope was silver, red, black, brown, yellow, and white. Mr. H. Myrrh picked up the rope and tugged on it.

"As you can see, this rope is very, very strong. No Lack hair in this rope. Their hair is slippery. Human hair is much better!"

Lilly was frightened and wanted to stall for time.

"Tell me, Mr. H. Myrrh, what's the 'H' for?" said Lilly, asking the first thing that came to mind.

"I thought you'd never ask," he proudly replied. "Take a guess."

"Howard?" Lilly guessed.

"Nope."

"Harry?"

He shook his head with amused disgust, loving every minute of this game.

"Okay…Henry? Heinrick? Hercules? Horatio?"

"Nah, wrong again, but keep guessing. I have plenty of time for guessing games," he said, rolling his eyes up in the air and tapping his foot with his arms crossed.

"Hank, Harvey, Haley, Hymen, Hal, Hilo . . . ," she went on and on.

"No! The *H* is for *Hugh*. Hugh Myrrh, get it?" he exploded! He couldn't hold it in anymore, laughing.

Lilly thought for a few seconds and then began to laugh. When she laughed, the sky lit up with thousands, maybe millions, of stars. Lilly jumped into the air. They had been there all along. She just needed to laugh. Mr. H. Myrrh caught her in mid-air, and she kissed his orange-pink dragon cheek as they danced around the Well of Unfathomable Suffering, laughing and laughing, making new piles of gold nuggets.

"Now it is time, Lilly," he said, "for you to go down into the Well."

He collected some of the new gold rocks and gave them to her to put in her pocket. He began to sing a riddle song while he uncoiled his hair rope. Lilly sat on the side of the wall of the Well with her feet dangling over the edge and looked way, way down into the darkness as she listened to him sing.

Here, silly Lilly, who couldn't guess my name,
But when she laughed and saw the stars,
Her life would never ever be the same.
So take this gold and when the time is right,

Throw it to the wind.
Most would think that foolish!
But it's the Fool who knows no gain.
It's the Fool who knows no blame.
So here, silly Lilly, take this gold,
And go merrily down the Well.
Know no fear, my little dear, my sweet silly Lilly!

He handed her the rope and started singing the tune again.

"Thank you for everything," said Lilly.

"My pleasure. Anytime. Well, except when I am sleeping. Never wake a sleeping desert dragon if you know what's good for you. But that's only once every century," he warned her.

"You only sleep once every hundred years?" she asked, astonished.

"Yep, get a lot done that way, a lot of tidying to do," he said, laughing, as he began to lower her down the Well on the colored-hair rope. Lilly laughed too, and more stars burst bright in the night sky.

"Okay, I'll remember that," she said, looking up at him from the Well and thinking he was probably kidding.

He started singing the riddle song again which echoed down into the Well. At first, the Well was brightly lit because of the crescent moon and stars shining on the gold lined walls, but then it got darker and darker as she went down farther and farther. After a while, she couldn't hear him singing anymore.

"Mr. Myrrh! Wait! Pull me up! I'm not ready," she called up toward the top of the Well, but she only heard her own voice echo.

"MR. H. MYRRH! Please answer me!" she yelled again, louder.

She hung on to the hair rope in the dark. She wondered how far down the water was. She wondered if there was any water in this well. She never asked him that. What would she land on? She should have asked. He probably wouldn't have told her anyway.

"Mr. Hugh Myrrh! Mr. Myrrh, please!"

She tried to remember Mr. H. Myrrh's riddle song to sing, but she couldn't. She couldn't remember any songs at all! Slowly, a great endless sadness entered her heart. Sorrow oozed over the air in through her pores. She wept. She heard sighing and moaning and crying in the distance.

Suddenly the hair rope dropped and Lilly screamed, hanging on as best she could.

Then the dropping stopped and Lilly hung suspended, barely breathing.

She heard water dripping nearby and a splash just like the sound the muskrat made in the creek back home at night. There were cries and moans closer now. The water swooshed but she couldn't see anything in the blackness of the Well.

"Hello? Who's there?" she called out.

"Oh, it could be Lacks. Don't say anything, Lilly," she whispered to herself.

Suddenly, she felt a strong tug on her left leg. The tug pulled her right off the rope. Down into the water she went with a splash. Underneath the water she saw a creature, the creature that had pulled her off the rope. It was narrow like a snake and about six feet long. It was glowing with copper, green and gold colors and had shining blue eyes and pointy copper-colored fins along its back. The creature had sparkling crystals on its head. It was beautiful and scary at the same time, and it lit up the water, a brilliant silver blue.

"I am not always here when someone comes down the Well of Unfathomable Suffering, but for you, Lilly, there is great beauty and mystery in the darkness that you fear and so you are here with me," it said. "You can breathe in the water of the Shimmering World. Take a breath."

Lilly did. She could breathe!

"Hold on to me tight," the creature said. "The strong currents could easily carry you away."

Lilly grabbed its tail and held on tight.

"How did you know my name?" she asked.

She could speak in the water too.

"I know all the children's names, and besides, King Myrrh sent word to me that you would be coming down the Well. I am Ninah, Queen of the Shimmering World."

"Is that where we are going?"

"We are there already," Ninah said, as she swam down swiftly on a diagonal.

They swam through the waters for sometime. As Lilly relaxed, she began to see fish all around her—fish of spectacular beauty and color. They said hello to her as they swam by, just like friendly people on city streets. They blew musical bubbles. She saw mermaids and mermen swimming along, playing and talking with brightly colored dolphins. The dolphins were rosy pink, silvery gray, sunflower yellow, tangerine orange, electric blue and apple green. They wore fragrant necklaces of underwater flowers and shells. Lilly and Ninah swam between huge rock formations made of emerald, sapphire and golden amber and covered with flowering flowing vines. Lilly heard unusual harmonious music that one could only ever hear in the deep, silver-blue water of the Shimmering World. She ate feasts of cool underwater fruit salads and warm sea-vegetable soup with the best yellow cornbread she had ever tasted. It was difficult to say how long she was there because time was very different here. After Lilly had eaten and rested, it was time to go.

"Hold onto me, Lilly," Ninah told her, as they began to swim upward.

"I love it here. I don't want to leave."

The Shimmering World never leaves you," Ninah told her as they swam.

Lilly could see light at the top as they came toward the surface. They popped up through the glittering silver water and Lilly took a breath of the air. She saw land far in the distance. Ninah was now swimming toward it.

"Where are we going? What is that land up ahead?" asked Lilly.

"Shhhh, Lilly, we must be silent," said Ninah in a whisper. "We must not talk right now. We are in the Silver Sea of Silence. This water is listening, the air is listening. This can be a dangerous place for noisy visitors. There are strong currents here, and if disturbed, they can pull you to where unfriendly creatures lurk about in a place where time can be from forever to never. Silence, now."

Lilly held on tight to Ninah and kept silent. As they got closer to land she saw a cove where the water began to turn turquoise blue. Ninah caught a little wave and they rode it to the shore. The sand was peach colored. It looked just like the cove that she had stood in when she visited Tu and The Fish on that snowy night. Ninah swam around Lilly and poked her head out of the water.

"We can talk now. This is the Peach Sand Cove."

"I've been here before with Tu and The Fish," Lilly told her. "Are they coming?"

"Patience, trust and courage for the one who wears the Shell," Ninah said and rose out of the water, kissing Lilly on the forehead.

Then Ninah dove away under the water. Lilly saw her shining copper fins surface farther from the beach and watched her for as long as she could. Lilly stood at the edge looking out over the water, waiting for Tu and The Fish to appear.

CHAPTER 6

Someone Unexpected

Beyond the beach was a thick tropical forest. Birds and little monkeys could be heard chirping and chattering in the dense woods. Lilly sat down on the peach colored sand, enjoying the warmth of the golden sun of this enchanted land. She lay back and closed her eyes, drifting off to sleep.

"Hello," she heard a voice say softly.

Opening her eyes, she saw a moth fluttering above her face.

"Oh, hello," said Lilly, surprised.

"My name is Ming Li. I am the companion of Princess Anais of Beetle Island. I can help you find the road."

The moth flew across the beach toward the edge of the forest.

"Follow me," she said.

Lilly stood up and followed her through lush blossoming trees and vines to a narrow path.

"Are we going to where Princess Anais is?" asked Lilly.

The moth turned. Her eyes were midnight blue. She had white wings. Little ruby-red and emerald-green jewels and swirls of color

covered her body. "No, Princess Anais is captive on her ship, The Lady Scarab. I was with her when she was taken."

Lilly gasped. Ming Li carried on.

"The Lack Moregrott climbed onto the ship with more than a hundred of his army of Lacks. They murdered the crew and threw them overboard."

"He wants the Magic Gown, doesn't he?" asked Lilly.

"Yes. He doesn't want you to have it or anyone else," replied the moth. "He screamed at the Princess, 'Give me the Magic Gown. I command you. It is mine and I take what I want!' She was wearing the gown at the time. He grabbed at the gown but was unable to touch it. His fingers began to cramp and curl in on themselves.

"'You cannot take what is not meant to be owned,' Princess Anais said to him. 'This gown is not meant for the hands of greed and hatred or your darkened heart that kills.'

"He tried again to take the gown but his fingers cramped once more. He leaned as close to the Princess as he could and said, 'I will take you down to the City of Grott where all you can do is rot.'

"'I don't think that will happen. The gown's magic is greater than your greed,' she replied to him.

"'Fear me,' Moregrott continued, 'fear me if you know what's good for you!'

"'I pity you,' she said back to him."

"Wow, she sounds so brave," said Lilly.

"She is very brave," said the moth. "After Moregrott tried one more time to take the gown, he commanded that she be taken to the hold of the ship. Before she was carried away, she said to me, 'Ming Li, fly across the Silver Sea and get word to my parents in the High Hibiscus Garden of what has happened. Tell them I've not seen Lilly and I'm protecting the Magic Gown. Go swiftly, my friend,' she said."

"Lilly," Ming Li whispered, "walk quickly."

"Why? What's wrong?" Lilly asked.

"I thought I heard something," said the moth." It may have been nothing but we should be careful."

"Heard what?" Lilly asked.

The moth's words became urgent, "Hurry, Lilly! Run!"

Lilly began to run. The air suddenly reeked with odors fouler than anything Lilly had ever smelled. Lilly started to gasp. Her chest began to ache. She heard heavy footsteps crunching through vegetation. She saw flowers wilting around her and colorful birds and small monkeys falling from the trees. Strange gurgling and growling noises came from close behind her as Lilly suddenly felt something grab her leg and pull her to the ground. She felt the color draining from her body. Lilly lay holding her chest. She remembered Mr. Myrrh's warning about the Lacks and realized nothing could have prepared her for what she now saw. Human-like forms dressed in people's clothes, with hats and jackets, swarmed around her and the moth. Their skin was transparent but mottled light gray and a sickly pale yellow. Instead of eyes, they had empty black holes that somehow sucked in color and life like a vacuum. They had little hair, but what they had was long, stringy and different colors, dirty colors of white and orange-brown and every nasty color in between. Their mouths were large and lipless and filled with pointed yellow teeth, like bats. The Lacks bent over Lilly and clawed at her with dirty broken nails. Lilly saw lice crawling through their hair and across their faces. She felt very sick. Ming Li fluttered, trying to scare them off, but soon she fell to the ground helpless, gasping. Her lovely colors faded to gray as the Lacks fixed their eyes on her. One of the Lacks lifted his hideous leg to stomp on the moth but abruptly froze in position as a loud humming sound grew from the forest.

Suddenly the air became green and blue. Hundreds of shimmering hummingbirds carrying yellow and white honeysuckle blossoms swarmed around the Lacks. The hummingbirds dropped honeysuckle nectar onto the Lacks, and as the nectar touched their skin, it burned right through it. They fell to the ground, wiggling like giant worms, growling and groaning and began to shriek and shrink. They shrank into small rectangular and square stones while others, untouched by the nectar, escaped, running into the forest. The hummingbirds flew around Lilly and Ming Li and then disappeared into the forest.

Lilly lay still, catching her breath. Once she felt her color coming back, she stood up and walked over to the moth. Ming Li lay on the ground, motionless, taking shallow little breaths. Lilly didn't know what to do and was wondering how to help when out from the trees flew a winged creature. A fairy, one of the rarest in the land, swooped in and stopped in an elegant manner beside Lilly and Ming Li. The fairy was part bird and part woman. She stood about two feet tall and was adorned in lavender, rosy pink and light-green feathers. Her face was soft pastel colors like her feathers. She wore a yellow buttercup flower on her fine, golden, curly hair and had large, dark brown liquid eyes. From a tiny pouch she dropped a golden liquid into the little moth's mouth, whispering something Lilly didn't understand. The fairy bird then flew to Lilly and placed a fragrant crown of honeysuckle blossoms on her head.

She whispered, "Go now and find the path. You have to go on your own from here."

The fairy bird lifted the little moth's limp body and disappeared into the thick forest. Lilly looked longingly after them but knew she had to go ahead alone.

Lilly hurried on through the forest and out the other side. Beyond the forest a lavender sky hung over a vast lavender land. As far as she could see, small bushes, moss-covered rocks, little pale-blue flowers and short purple grasses decorated the landscape. Lilly walked out onto the violet ground.

She walked for many hours, looking for some kind of signs of a road, but saw nothing. As she walked, the sky became a darker color of purple, as if some kind of nighttime was occurring. After some time, Lilly couldn't see very well and thought maybe she should find a moss-covered rock and sleep against it for a while, hoping no Lacks would find her. She curled up behind one of the bigger boulders.

Lilly didn't rest very well. The thought of the Lacks coming upon her was frightening. It was dawn when she decided to walk again. She started out, singing the lullaby and trying to remember the words of Mr. H. Myrrh's song. Suddenly she felt uneasy, tingling with goose bumps and butterflies. Soon the smell of Lacks confirmed what she saw through the gloom: Lacks creeping from behind the big boulders. They were coming at her from all directions. Wherever they stepped, color disappeared from that place. Purple faded to gray. Their black vacuum eyes drained all vibrant colors from the land. Lilly ran. The honeysuckle crown flew off her head. A big Lack crushed it but he screeched in pain when he touched the flowers and shriveled into a stone. Lacks were everywhere. Lilly was surrounded. The Lacks moved in closer. They clawed at her. They drooled from their putrid mouths. Lilly felt ill. Her knees wobbled and gave out. Nearby, a group of Lacks were pushing a huge boulder. When they finally rolled it over, Lilly saw a giant hole in the ground. The Lacks pulled her down into the hole.

As Lilly dropped into it, she drifted delirious into a nightmare world. The air was heavy, like a wet dirty blanket, and she retched from the stench of the Lacks. She fell in and out of consciousness as they carried her down, down, down. Through her delirium, she could hear screams and crying, metal grinding and digging sounds. She woke shivering, lying on a cold wet carpet. Her head felt so heavy she could barely lift it. Lilly opened her eyes slowly to see a creature lying on a filthy old couch. Its eyeless sockets were closed, and a bony bruised arm covered in gaudy gold jewelry dangled near Lilly. Lilly moved away from the dangling arm, but the creature clutched her by the hair.

"Where do you think you're going, little one with the pretty hair?" said a gurgling woman's voice.

"Look at me," she pulled Lilly's hair. "Look at me! Queen Merciles of Grott is talking to you and asking you, why is the queen Lack wearing an old gown stolen from a grave?"

"I don't know," answered Lilly, weakly.

"Stupid girl!"

A faded and stained pink velvet and green embroidered dress hung off the creature's transparent, pale, skinny body. The hideous queen stroked her long dirty thin hair, and when a clump of it fell out into her hand, she threw it at Lilly. Lilly pulled it from her cheek, trying not to be sick.

Queen Merciles pulled Lilly close to her. "Tell me, you little runt of a girl, you will get the Magic Gown for me, won't you?"

Lilly shook her head and thought of Princess Anais. "No, I can't. You're not kind. You're mean."

"What? Ukkkk! Don't make me sick with that word 'kind.' Ukkkk!" Merciles said. "Who told you that, the little moth I killed?"

"She's not dead . . ." Lilly cried and retched.

Up close, Lilly could see lice crawling across her face and she fainted. Merciles shook her, pulling at her hair.

"Wake up! You're being a little wise guy, huh? Funny girl! We'll see how funny you can be."

Lilly woke up. Merciles pulled the girl toward her.

"Get me the Magic Gown! If you don't, I will do to you what has already been done to your friend," she warned her, handing Lilly a box.

"Open it!" she ordered.

Lilly opened the box.

"No!" Lilly cried.

She picked up the lifeless blue jay and held it to her cheek. Lilly stroked the bird's feathers, crying. As she held the poor bird, Lilly suddenly got the strength to be angry, angrier than she'd ever been in her whole life.

"You killed him and he never hurt anyone or anything!" Lilly screamed. "You killed J!"

Queen Merciles laughed, "Stupid bird! Stupid girl! I do what I want to get what I want!

"Now, let me see that shell you're wearing," and she went to grab the necklace from around Lilly's neck.

Lilly pushed back from her, but a huge Lack grabbed her from behind.

"No, leave me alone! Magic is all around me!" Lilly yelled.

"Oh, I can see that. What a joke that is! Then bring your little bird back! Ha, ha, ha, ha, ha," Merciles laughed cruelly in Lilly's face, "no one can help you now, not even that fat old dragon!" She grabbed the blue jay from Lilly's hand and quickly swallowed it whole.

"See, I ate your magic. I've stolen your magic. Yummmm, your little blue-feathered friend tastes so good," Merciles brutally teased.

"You cruel, ugly, disgusting monster! You can't eat the magic! I hope you choke on J!"

Queen Merciless laughed, "Oh, aren't we the defiant one, little brat!"

She began to choke a little. Lilly refused to speak.

"Angry are we, little girl? Stubborn, too. I've got the thing for you: the Squirms Pit! Take her away to my babies! Take her to the Squirms Pit. You will love my pretty, hungry little squirms, but better yet, they will love you . . . for dinner."

The Lacks began to drag her out of the room.

"Help, someone! Please! Mr. Myrrh!"

"That old stupid dragon, what's he going to do?" Merciles mocked.

"Wait," she yelled, "not with that shell necklace. You won't be needing that where you're going."

Lilly suddenly heard the dragon's voice singing in her stomach; she heard Mr. H. Myrrh sing, *"So take this gold and when the time is right, throw it to the wind."*

Lilly put her hand to her stomach and felt the gold nuggets the dragon had given her in her pocket. She took the rocks and threw them all at the queen. One went right down her throat and she began choking and gasping for air.

"Ahhhhkkk!" gasped the Queen. "Ahhhhkkk!"

The other gold rocks flew into the air, shimmering and glowing and now turning into hundreds of bright goldfinches, swarming like a golden swirling cloud. They surrounded Lilly and lifted her off the ground. The Lacks scrambled to find her in the cloud of yellow birds, but Lilly was soaring through the tunnel at lightning speed.

"J!" called Lilly out loud.

Lilly rose to the opening in the ground and burst out into the air.

CHAPTER 7

The Next Places

The finches carried her quickly over the lavender terrain. Lilly began to see small creatures like rabbits and squirrels moving about and knew she was safe for a while. She saw deer grazing on the lavender grasses and up ahead she saw a road.

The goldfinches carried her to the road and placed her gently on the surface. The road went on and on over rolling hills. As Lilly came to the top of the highest hill, she saw the most majestic tree she had ever seen. It was enormous, wider than a house. Soft, pink, velvet moss was growing on the dark brown bark and small pink blossoms filled the branches. Honeybees buzzed around the blossoms. Near the ground the tree was covered with green moss, ivy and small blue flowers. Four blue and purple steps led to an open blue door right in the middle of the trunk of the tree. Lilly climbed the stairs and stepped into the entrance room.

"Hello?" Lilly called.

"Point of no return," she heard a nearby voice say.

A thin little brown man with feathers in his hair and light blue eyes leaned out from behind the door. Lilly jumped.

"Point of no return," he repeated.

"What?" she blurted.

"This is the Springtree, the point of no return for all visitors," he said again, dancing around the room.

"Oh. And who are you?" she asked.

"Who am I? What a question!" he said, dancing and spinning. "Why, I am Stee-Ven, the Dancing Tree Man." Then he stopped very close to her, saying, "And who, might I ask, are you?"

"Lilly," she replied.

"Oh yes, Lilly, with the Shell of Great Fortune and Mysterious Ways. Welcome! Come dance with me, Lilly," he said, as he took her hand and twirled her around.

"No, I don't want to dance," she cried, pulling away. "Queen Merciless killed J."

"She is no queen. Make no mistake about that! Now, don't you believe everything you hear, sweet child." He took her in his arms.

"But she killed J, my friend. I saw it," she cried harder.

"Oh, dear! I am sorry indeed." Stee-Ven held her close and gently swayed from side to side. "You are in the right place for your sorrow."

Out from his pocket he pulled the tiniest little honey jar and opened it. "Taste this."

Lilly touched the golden honey with her finger and tasted it. It was the most delicious honey she had ever had. "Hmmmm, that's good."

"The best in all the lands," he smiled, wiping her tears. "It was quite an accomplishment, you finding the Springtree all by yourself," he said encouragingly.

"With the help of magic of course," Lilly smiled.

"Oh, but of course! It is nice to see you smiling. Would you like some more?"

Lilly took another taste of the honey.

"You know, the Springtree is the place of many of the great secrets."

"What secrets?" she asked.

"The really good ones," he whispered, playfully leaning closer.

He put the little honey jar back in his pocket and turned Lilly around. Before her, in the center of the room, she saw a sparkling crystal spiral staircase going up through the tree as far as she could see.

"That wasn't there before!" she exclaimed.

"Come on, Lilly," he said, taking her hand. They started up the crystal stairs.

As they climbed, he told her stories of ancient times and of visitors of all kinds that had come to the Springtree. He said he had been part of this tree since the beginning.

Sometimes he spoke a few words in an unusual language, like King Rue. Lilly repeated the foreign words to herself, trying to remember them, but there were so many things he was telling her that she had a hard time keeping all his stories straight.

"Is this a really far away place, Stee-Ven," she asked, "so far away I can't get home again, or is this like a dream place, not real?"

He laughed. "Now that's a question! A dream place is certainly a real place, and we are not a faraway place at all," he said, as he pointed to her heart. "It's just a bit tricky to find us, like a great adventure. But it seems you have, and many others have too."

Lilly stopped climbing the stairs. "Really? Who?"

"Let's see, I suppose I could start in alphabetical order . . . but that would take forever. Well, not too long ago there was a ballerina, a bus driver, an astronomer, a grandmother, and a . . ." Stee-Ven noticed a peach, pink and gold colored mist swirling, surrounding them. "We must keep climbing; we're almost there."

"Oh, look!" Lilly ran up a few steps ahead to where the stairs ended at a black-iron scrolled gate, like a garden gate. Beyond it, more mist swirled and there was nothing.

"Where are we?" she asked him.

"Hmmm, it seems we are at the Next Place, the place of your own creation."

Lilly heard a high-pitched sound, EEEEEEEEEE, coming from the depths of the mist. She looked around and could not see her companion anywhere.

Rubyrock Falls

High
Hibiscus
Garden

Red Tree Forest

Blue Tree
Forest

Deep Blue River

The Land
of King Joseph

The
Celestial

Rose
Garden

The Next Place

Honeybee
Cove

Springtree
Honey

"Where are you?" she called.

"Right here," he called from the mist and came closer to her.

"Lilly, we are at the Next Place at the right time for you, your time, and things must keep moving as they always have, just like in the river and the ocean you like to kayak in."

"How do you know that?"

"I'm not so far away, remember?"

"You're coming with me, aren't you?" she asked.

From over his head he took off a little pouch and strung it around her neck.

"For you."

"What is this?"

"It's the Springtree honey," he smiled and laughed.

"What's so funny?"

"You'll see later, a secret."

A sound shook the stairs, EEEEEEEEEEE. The iron gate began to vibrate.

"Do you have anything else you want to know?" he asked her.

"Why, where are you going?"

"Back to the tree. I must," he said.

"No, don't leave me! Where am I going?"

EEEEEEEEEEEEEEE! The sound vibrated the whole tree. EEEEEEEEEEEEEEEEEEE! Lilly felt it going through her body. EEEEEEEEEEEEEEEEEEEEEEEEE!

"The gate's not open! How do I open the gate?"

"A very good question, but you already have the answer to that," he told her.

"No, I don't." Lilly felt butterflies in her stomach.

"Lilly, everything will be okay!"

She turned to talk to Stee-Ven, but he wasn't there anymore. The tree and the crystal staircase were disappearing, too, from below. The sound was even louder now, EEEEEEEEEEEEEEE! Lilly pulled and pushed at the gate. She heard herself say, "Open! Open! Hurry!"

Nothing happened.

EEEEEEEEEEEEEEEEEEE!

The stairway was disappearing; soon it would be gone altogether.

She tried to calm herself. She whispered, "Please, gate, my name is Lilly. I carry the honey of the Springtree and wear the Shell of Great Fortune and Mysterious Ways. Please open so that I may pass to the Next Place."

The gate creaked and began to open.

She stepped through the opening into the mist just as the stairs disappeared from under her feet and the tree was gone.

The feeling of butterflies in her stomach got worse.

She thought she heard the sound of grumbling or gurgling. Then she smelled the awful scent of Lacks.

Oh, no, this can't be happening now. Not after all this! "Stee-Ven!"

She could see the dark shadows of their figures in the mist around her. Her heart began to ache and she could hardly breathe. Her color was draining fast. There were hundreds of them.

"How could I have come this far and not make it? I can't get caught by Merciles again." She clutched the shell and the honey pouch around her neck.

The Lacks came closer to her and she struggled to run, like in a dream when you just can't move.

A rosy red butterfly fluttered in front of her face, practically landing on her nose.

It was the butterfly from the colorful wind. "Theresa! Can you help me? What do I do?"

Lilly fell to the ground. "It's hopeless," she cried. "I can't do this, I can't!"

"Remember, Lilly," said Theresa. "Remember what Stee-Ven said."

"But he said so much," said Lilly.

"About the Next Place," Theresa replied, "a place of your own creation. What does it look like to you? What will you create? Think Lilly."

Lilly closed her eyes. She imagined all the Lacks turning into rectangular and square stones like they did in the forest.

"Open your eyes, Lilly," Theresa exclaimed.

Lilly saw the Lacks shriveling into hundreds of stones just like she had imagined them. Some tried to run but they all became stones. The rocks started to pile on top of one another, building a wall. A wooden arched doorway appeared in the wall. The Lacks were gone. They were stones that made the wall. Flowers and ivy quickly grew up the wall, covering the Lack stones. Theresa was smiling and flying around.

"What a magnificent idea!" the butterfly exclaimed.

Lilly touched the stones and smelled the flowers.

"It is beautiful," Lilly said.

Theresa fluttered up and down the stone wall. The arched doorway in the center was open.

"Oh, look, Lilly . . ." the butterfly called, flying through the doorway.

"Hey, wait for me, Theresa." Lilly followed her.

On either side of the doorway stood two very tall, old, red rosebud trees like sentinel guardians. Beyond, Lilly could see a rose garden filled with the blossoms like the ones in her living room at home. The air was sweet with the fragrance of the flowers. Honeybees and butterflies flew from blossom to blossom. From the sky, colorful flowers fell softly like raindrops, landing in her hair and on the ground.

"Lilly, you've done it! Theresa exclaimed. "You are in the Land of King Joseph, the kindest king that ever was. Look!"

Down a path through the center of the garden, a blue elephant walked slowly and majestically toward them, swinging his blue trunk and flapping his large blue ears.

"Hello, Lilly, my name is Joseph. Welcome to this land," he trumpeted, in a deep but soft voice.

Hello," she replied and bowed to him without even thinking of it. His face was truly regal. His voice was lovely, like the deepest melody Lilly had ever heard. *If ever there was a king, he would be him*, Lilly thought.

"Have you ever ridden a blue elephant before?" he asked.

"No," she replied, "not even a gray elephant."

"Well, get on, my friend, and enjoy the ride," he said, as he bowed and tucked his front legs under him so that Lilly could climb on his back.

"You too," he said to Theresa, and the red butterfly sat on top of his head between his big flopping ears. He walked along a path that was just wide enough for his body. He began to climb a steep path upward as he sang a song about a singing mountain and a hidden lake.

They came to a clearing like a small garden, with a bright pink table and three blue chairs. On the table sat a large golden cup. Joseph knelt

down to the ground and Lilly slid from his back, laughing and giddy. She sat in one of the chairs, leaning over to peek into the big golden cup. "What's in there?"

"The water from the river in the Blue Tree Forest can only be found here," he said, and handed her the cup with his trunk. "You must be thirsty, little one; changing Lacks into stones will do that. Well done!" he laughed.

"I am thirsty. Thank you."

Lilly took the cup and drank it. It was delicious, refreshing, cool water. Suddenly, as if shimmering through a mirage, a door appeared behind the table.

"Come, Lilly, let us visit the land beyond this door," he said calmly. Lilly was no longer nervous.

He walked her through the doorway. Theresa sat on the top of his head.

A bright blue tree appeared and then another and another; it was a forest of blue trees with pink blossoms and glowing green leaves. Vines of purple and red leaves grew up along the trees trunks like colorful necklaces. All around were flowerbeds, and the ground changed color from pale blue to yellow to green. A dark blue river flowed down the center of the landscape. Lilly stood next to Joseph on the riverbank and watched the water swirl and dance.

Joseph sang in his deep beautiful voice:

> *"Created by the up above,*
> *the sky so blue to see.*
> *Created by the down below,*
> *the velvet grass so green to me.*
> *Created with the moving earth,*
> *the river always giving birth,*
> *to those who trace the endless sky,*
> *who mark the earthy floor.*
> *Watch closely the river's dance!*
> *Her words are hidden with simple glance!*

And if by chance she lets you know,
  the secrets learned so long ago.
Remember, you are very few,
  the river let the light come through!"

"Whose secrets, Joseph? Yours?"

"No, my dear, the river's secrets."

"I wish I knew them," Lilly said.

"You already do. It's the magic all around us, it's the magic that brought you here, and it's the magic that's inside you."

Then, as they walked, a bright red tree appeared in front of them as if it had marched out of the forest.

"Wow!" said Lilly.

And then another red tree, and another. "The magic gets very strong now. We are in the Red Tree Forest," he whispered.

"Where King Rue and Mik are from!"

They walked along a path which began to climb upward past a waterfall cascading over ruby red rocks covered with flowers and vines. Red birds and tiny winged creatures played in the waterfalls. Hibiscus flowers were everywhere.

"We are here," said Joseph. "Look up."

Above her, two huge, brilliantly colored tropical eagles sat on the hibiscus branches. The blossoms framed them like royal canopies. The birds spread their wings and lifted off the branches, gracefully floating to the ground in front of her. They transformed before Lilly's wide eyes. The smaller bird shimmered into a woman of magnificent beauty who still resembled the bird she was moments before. Her dress was the color of her feathers. Her hair, long and feathery, was in shades of brown and gold, like autumn.

The larger bird was now a handsome man with long dark hair, golden brown skin and captivating amber eyes. In his right hand he held a tall, wooden, spiraled staff with feathers and crystals on it.

The smaller bird spoke first.

"Hello, Lilly. I am White Tears and this is Cameo, the ninth king of the Land of Ten Kings and Roses. Princess Anais is our daughter."

"Hello, Lilly," the king said and bowed. "I greet you as the one who wears the Shell of Great Fortune and Mysterious Ways with great courage."

Lilly was in awe in their company. Barely catching her breath, she could not speak. Joseph affectionately wrapped his trunk around her.

"You're doing great, little one," he whispered.

White Tears walked close to Lilly, touched her shoulder and gently stroked her cheek with a feathery touch.

"Yes, dear one, it is your courage and your destiny that have brought you here to us. We did not intend it to be so difficult to give you what is meant for your world right now."

"The Magic Gown? The Magic Gown that the Lacks are after?" asked Lilly.

"Yes, the Magic Gown; Princess Anais was to give it to you that night in the Peach Sand Cove, but the selfish greed of Moregrott and Merciles changed that. They think magic can be harshly taken. We are sorry for the trouble and the danger the Lacks have caused you."

Cameo spoke, "The Magic Gown must go to your world; the time has come. It is not meant for here anymore. It has traveled far for many years."

"The Magic Gown was given to me a long time ago by the King and Queen of the Colorful Wind," White Tears told her. "When Cameo and I came here from a star in the Realm of the Colorful

Wind, we brought with us a piece of our star, three colors of water—silver, green and gold—the rose seeds and the special honeybees. That is how the Land of Ten Kings began."

"If you are wondering why you are here, it is because we are your ancestors and you carry our magic. You, like us, are a star traveler. Part bird, flower, human and star, you carry this in your blood for many generations on your mother's side."

"A star traveler?" Lilly asked, overwhelmed.

"Yes. That's why you came to visit us on Beetle Island when you were a little girl. Princess Anais wanted to meet you. That is why you wear the twin Shell of our daughter, Princess Anais. It is you who must find her and the Magic Gown. Only a star traveler from your world can make this journey, not us."

"There are other star travelers where I come from?" Lilly asked.

"Yes, and they are remembering," White Tears told her.

Cameo placed his hand on the top of Lilly's head. "The door has opened. Rest here tonight with us, but in the morning you must go north to the Butterfly Cliffs and farther on to the Wild Land of Skree, where Moregrott is taking Princess Anais. Take my staff. It will help you."

He handed her the tall wooden staff.

Theresa fluttered around Lilly and then landed on the top of the staff.

"Look for the cedar stump; there you will find your direction," Cameo told her.

"Know that our hearts have always been with you and always will be," Lilly heard White Tear's beautiful voice say.

They both bowed their heads to Lilly, then, together, transformed back into tropical eagles and flew from the ground. They soared high above the branches. Lilly watched them as they began to encircle each other in the higher currents. Two feathers fell from the sky before they flew beyond her vision.

"They have honored you with their precious feathers. It is a great omen," said Joseph. "A great omen, indeed."

Lilly picked the feathers up and followed Joseph to a room made of roses. Inside was a soft evergreen pine bed. Lilly lay down on the bed and was immediately asleep. The next morning, Lilly tied the two feathers into the back of her hair and followed King Joseph and Theresa to the far reaches of the High Hibiscus Garden. At the edge of the path was a clearing that looked out over a vast expanse of open land.

Pointing with his trunk, Joseph instructed, "Out there are the Butter-fly Cliffs. Find the pass that goes between them. It will take you to the forest where the cedar stump is."

Lilly stepped from the path carrying the staff. The scent of lavender and rosemary was in the air. Soft gray clouds lay overhead as if it may rain soon. She turned and saw the majestic blue elephant, with Theresa sitting on his head, bidding her farewell. "I'm on my own now," she said to herself, "but I have you with me, don't I, staff?"

She walked for days, resting when the dark came, sleeping on the ground on soft beds of lavender brush. She ate small amounts of honey from the pouch as she walked. She smiled and laughed when she realized what secret Stee-Ven was laughing about when he gave her the honey pouch: the honey never ran out! The little pouch was always replenished with more honey when she opened it. What happy honey.

The clouds thickened, the rain began to fall and the ground began to get steeper. Lilly climbed higher.

At the same time, to the northwest, beyond land in the Dark Green Ocean of Fortune, The Lady Scarab with Princess Anais aboard sailed north toward the Wild Land of Skree.

CHAPTER 8

On The Lady Scarab

As The Lady Scarab sailed through the night, Princess Anais sat below deck. She was tied to a beam, held by ropes. Even in the darkness of the cabin, Princess Anais was striking to look at. Her hair was long and dark, with a hint of midnight like the night sky. Her skin was a bronze color and her eyes were golden brown, like the color of the enchanted fruitwood on Beetle Island. On her head, woven into her hair, sat a crown of braided fruitwood with amber and emerald jewels. Princess Anais wore the Magic Gown, a long white dress with tiny pale blue flowers on it. Around her neck hung an oyster shell necklace like Lilly's.

Suddenly, quietly and steadily, the door handle turned. The cabin door opened inward very slowly, then a dark haired boy slipped through the opening and closed the door behind him. He hurried over to Anais and began to untie her wrists.

"Hello," said the boy. "My name is Tom Finch. I've been hiding on this ship all this time. I didn't know you were here until recently. I've been trying to get down here."

"I'm Princess Anais . . ."

The door handle turned again.

"Quick, hide!" she told him.

Tom hid behind a chest as a Lack came into the room.

"Who you talkin' to?" it gurgled. "I heard something."

The Lack approached Princess Anais, and as he did so, the Magic Gown glowed in shimmering pink, blue, green and lavender. Frightened, the Lack quickly backed away.

"Ah, never mind. Just you shut up, ya hear?"

"Soon that will be ours," he said, pointing to the dress.

The Lack slammed the door shut. Tom rushed to her again and began to untie her wrists.

"Wow, that's some dress. I've got to get you untied. I saw a small boat on deck; we'll try for it or else we'll jump overboard."

The door flew open quickly. It opened too quickly for Tom to react. Moregrott and two big Lacks entered the cabin.

"Well, well, look what we have here, a little hero! A surprise. A human boy. Now we have two brats!" Moregrott grabbed Tom and held him down.

"Where did you come from, boy? Don't be tellin' me tales either, or these two will have you for dinner, ripped in two pieces."

Moregrott picked him fully off the ground. He smelled deadly and Tom grew pale. His chest ached badly.

"Leave him alone, Moregrott!" Princess Anais demanded.

"A friend of yours, bug?" he mocked her.

Moregrott dropped Tom to the ground. Tom hit his head hard and fell unconscious.

"Tie him up away from the little bug princess," Moregrott commanded them. They dragged his body to the other beam.

He looked into her face, getting as close as he could.

"And you, missy Princess, what do you know about this? We're sailing north. I want to go south, to Grott! You know that. The wind and currents seem to have a mind of their own. What spell is this you and that dress have cast? You better break it or else . . ." Moregrott punched the wall with his fist. "You know what swims near the cliffs of the Wild Land of Skree don't you, little bug? The great green sharks swim there lookin' for food."

Moregrott and the Lacks left the room.

"Tom," Anais called, "Tom, open your eyes."

Tom stirred and opened his eyes.

"Those things are the Lacks, aren't they?"

"Yes."

"The dragon told me about them. When I came on board that first night, I couldn't see them but I sure could smell them."

"You've met the dragon?" Princess Anais asked, excited. "I've never been to the Great Desert. When did you meet him?"

"I don't know how long ago it was, but it was in the summer when I went out on my boat and followed the silver current. That dragon, he was somethin' else! He was great."

"You got here by the silver current? Wow, that's difficult to find!" she said, surprised. "Tell me, Tom. Tell me how you got here."

"On the Star-Gazer, my boat. I motored up the river at dawn out into the ocean."

"Your boat has a motor? You are from the other world! But you must be a magic boy to get here." "Well, I don't know about that."

"What happened then, Tom?" she asked.

"I was motoring along and, like I said, I noticed a shimmering silver current, so I followed it into the ocean. I could see land up ahead and then, behind me, suddenly there was no land at all. I had been that far out in the ocean many times, but I had never seen this before. I should have been able to see the twin lighthouses near the inlet and the New York skyline to the north, but they were gone."

"New York," Princess Anais repeated. "Would I like it there?"

Tom laughed, "Sure, it's a great city."

"I grew up on Beetle Island; I don't know a city like that, Tom." Princess Anais smiled and said, "Tell me more!"

"Well, it began to get dark, so I headed for the mysterious land up ahead. I beached on the shore of a vast desert. I walked for days in the desert, except it was always night. I have no idea how long it was, but I do know I ate the last of my peanut butter sandwiches."

"Would I like peanut butter sandwiches?"

"Definitely!"

"Then what? You met the dragon?"

"Not right away. I found a trail of golden rocks and an occasional skeleton. I was getting very thirsty and hungry when I saw a glowing light coming from the ground in the distance. It was a well with golden walls."

"Oh, the Well of Unfathomable Suffering!"

"Yeah, that's the one. Next to the Well was a colorful rope made out of hair."

"A hair rope!" Princess Anais scrunched her face.

"I attached my water bottle to this rope and lowered it far down into the Well. I filled it with water and drank it and lowered it again. I was hungry but happy for the water. I sat next to the Well and had some rest. For a while, I stayed there drinking the water and waiting. I was hoping someone might come by with something to eat."

"Were you very frightened?" asked the Princess.

"Funny that, I wasn't really scared. I was just interested, that's all, and hungry! And it was interesting. As I sat there, I saw a shadow

A Map of
the Land of
Ten Kings and Roses

Silver
Mists

Silver Current to the Silver Mists

to the Shimmering Worlds

The City of Grot

Hair
Rope

Well of Un-
fathomable
suffering

(Way, way down there)

Ocean

Silver Current of the Crescent Moon

Great
Desert
of Uncertainty

crossing the moon. It crossed back and forth across the moon, then flew toward me. Next thing I knew, a giant flying dragon landed almost on top of me as if he didn't even see me. I jumped out of the way the last second."

"The one and only Mr. H. Myrrh!" Anais smiled.

"Yeah, that was him," Tom answered, and began to mimic the dragon: "'Well, haven't seen anyone like you at the Well in a long time. How ya' doing, kid? Came from the far reaches of the desert, did ya? By way of the rare silver current of the crescent moon? Not many people know that way, you know. I'm impressed, kid. I'm impressed.'"

Princess Anais laughed.

"The dragon spit this gold liquid every time he talked. It congealed into the golden rocks in the desert. He pushed me with his big finger and knocked me over. 'Where am I?' I asked him."

Tom mimicked the dragon's voice again. "'Well, let's just say you hit the lucky jackpot, kid; you are in the Great Desert of Uncertainty and I am Mr. H. Myrrh and this is the Well of Unfathomable Suffering.'" Tom leaned back on the beam. "And that's how I met the dragon."

"And he called that lucky," Princess Anais laughed.

"That's exactly what I said, and I asked him would it take me home to New Jersey."

"'Never heard of it, kid,' he said to me. 'This is the Well of Unfathomable Suffering! Care to jump in?' 'Do I have a choice?' I asked him. Then he started talking in dragon riddles.

"'Of course, my boy, you have a choice. What appears to be a choice is no choice at all. And with no choice at all, it is better to choose than to not choose. Whatever you want, in other words. What is meant to happen will happen. So make a choice, my boy! And watch what happens!'"

Anais's eyes opened wide. "Did you go down the Well, Tom? What did you choose?"

"Well, first the dragon fed me. He handed me a gold nugget and all of a sudden I was holding a yellow pear. It was so sweet and juicy! He gave me another nugget and it turned into a loaf of warm golden corn bread, and then another nugget became yellow delicious cheese. He's quite the magician!"

"'Feel free to stay as long as you like, kid,' he said, 'but I got a feeling you'll be on your way.'

'I should be getting home,' I replied. He laughed at me with that one.

'Oh, you'll get where you need to go down there, that's for sure, but first you must guess my first name.'"

"I stared at the dragon, thinking. 'Hugh,' I said."

"Wow, great guess, Tom," said Anais.

"That's what the dragon said," replied Tom. "I laughed and the black sky burst with thousands of twinkling bright stars."

"'So,' I said to him, 'it looks like I'm ready to go; I have to pitch on Saturday.'"

"Pitch on Saturday?" queried the Princess.

"Oh, so you don't know baseball either," Tom smiled at Anais. "That's exactly what the dragon said: 'What's "pitch on Saturday" mean?'"

"If we ever get out of this mess, I'll teach you like I taught Mr. Myrrh."

"You taught the King of the Great Desert of Uncertainty baseball, whatever that is?"

"Yes," said Tom. "I took a big old leg bone from the ground and gave it to Mr. Myrrh. I took one of the small gold nuggets and threw it at the bone, telling him to hit it."

"'Ready,' I shouted, 'here it comes!' and threw the gold rock to him. He swung the bone and WHACK! He hit the gold rock first time, and it flew high into the air. 'Wow, that's great!' I said. 'You're a natural-born hitter, Mr. Myrrh.'"

"Sounds like fun," said Anais.

"Oh, it was," said Tom. "Once he got the hang of it, he jumped around giving me gold rocks to pitch at him. Finally, after at least fifty pitches, the dragon said, 'How about I pitch to you?' So I took the leg bone and waited for the dragon to throw one. WHIFF! I swung the bone, but missed."

"'And you're a natural pitcher too! We could use you on our baseball team back home,' I said. The dragon threw a fast one and SMACK! This time I hit it far…far enough to be a home run at my field. I dropped the bone and ran around the Well and came sliding in at Mr. Myrrh's huge purple feet."

Anais laughed.

"Then we sat by the Well, and I explained what a baseball game was and how to play. We ate more pears, cheese and corn bread, all made from more of the gold baseballs.

"'I like this baseball, kid. I hope you get to pitch on Saturday,' said the dragon. 'Now it's time to go.' He handed me some gold rocks and told me to fill my water bottle when I got into the Well. The dragon took the hair rope and handed it to me.

"'See ya around, kid,' he said. 'Thanks, Hugh,' I called back. And that was the last I saw of the dragon king," said Tom, finally.

"So is that how you got here?" asked Princess Anais. "Down the Well of Unfathomable Suffering?"

"Yes," said Tom. "I took the rope as far down as I could go; then I just let go and I fell and fell for the longest time. Finally I hit water right into another silver current. I expected it to take me to my boat, but all I found was a big piece of driftwood. Clinging to it, I sort of fell asleep and drifted with the current for a very long time. I really thought I was going home until, 'clunk,' I hit the side of this boat and knew it wasn't mine."

"Oh, I am sorry you didn't get home," said the Princess, "but I am happy that you're here with me. A lot of terrible things can happen in the Well of Unfathomable Suffering. Only someone who is true to their destiny can come through the Well. You have a destiny; you are here for a reason."

Tom smiled at Princess Anais.

"Well, I don't know about that, but if my destiny is to rescue you from those horrible Lacks, then I will somehow," he promised.

"Tom, this dress is very special and has its own destiny. That's all I can tell you . . ."

Suddenly the door burst open again and Moregrott was inches from Anais's face.

Tom tried to break free.

"The cliffs are in sight! The sharks are near and hungry. Give me the gown and save yourself. Maybe I'll even let the boy live!"

They heard the winds howl and felt the ship leaning to one side.

A Lack walked into the room.

"Untie these two and bring them up!" Moregrott ordered.

Moregrott raced up the stairs shouting, "Drop the sails! Drop the sails, you wretched bunch of rotting corpses!"

Falling over each other, they pulled on the ropes and the yellow sails fell all at once. The ship slowed and drifted close to the cliffs, rocking back and forth in the choppy green waters.

"Anchor! Anchor! Drop the anchor, you lice-ridden mongrels!"

Two Lacks rushed to drop the anchor from the bow of the ship. The two Lacks fell overboard when the boat rocked, and within seconds a huge dark shadow came up from under them and devoured them, pulling them under.

"Anchor the ship!" Moregrott screamed. "And bring them to me!" A tall skinny Lack brought Anais and Tom to Moregrott. Then Moregrott pushed the Lack overboard, and the shadow rose from the depths and pulled him down with its teeth while the Lack screamed for its life.

"See what's out there? Change your mind about the gown, did you?"

Princess Anais didn't answer.

Tom saw a wave rising up from the sea. He knew it would hit the ship in less than a minute. It hit and he held steady. As the ship rocked, it knocked Moregrott over. Moregrott grabbed for Princess Anais. The gown glowed. Tom pulled Princess Anais away from Moregrott and moved to the edge of the ship. Moregrott lunged at them and caught a corner of the gown, but his hands cramped in pain. "It's mine!" he screamed.

Moregrott grabbed at Tom's leg. His grip was so strong it felt like he could snap Tom's leg in two. Tom looked around and saw a pointy broken piece of wood from one of the crates lying on the deck. He stretched to reach it, grabbed the wood and jabbed it hard into Moregrott's neck. The creature screeched, as dark oily blood oozed from the puncture. He grabbed at his bleeding neck, letting Tom go. Lacks were coming along the deck toward them. Tom and Anais jumped into the water.

Lacks piled into the ocean after them, but the huge sharks devoured them one by one. They could hear Moregrott screaming over the crashing of the water against the rocks. Tom knew they would be coming for them soon. Tom and Anais swam for the rocks as fast as they could.

Moregrott saw Anais's crown floating in the water and grabbed it in rage. Meanwhile, Tom found a flat rock and pushed Anais up onto it and climbed up after her. A wave crashed against the rock and the green water sprayed them as a Lack leaped from the water toward them, grabbing onto Anais and the gown with its claws. From below the water, a shadow appeared under the Lack. The shark rose out of the water and its black eyes looked right at Tom.

"I think that shark winked at me," he said, shocked.

The fish pulled hard at the Lack and gobbled it up with its razor sharp teeth as black oily blood bubbled up from the water. Tom helped Anais to her feet, and they started to climb toward a rocky canyon that went to a plateau on top of the cliffs. Below, they could see Moregrott angrily waving Anais's crown in the air at them while more than fifty Lacks scrambled to climb the cliffs. Some fell into the water. The shadows of the hungry Lack-eating sharks lurked below them.

Once on top, they could see the Lacks and Moregrott scurrying and screaming down below on The Lady Scarab, frightened to get off in fear of the great green sharks. As they walked, Anais's stomach growled loudly. Tom reached in his pocket and pulled out a gold rock and placed it in her hand. All of a sudden she was holding a sweet yellow pear.

"You are a magician too!"

"Not really."

"Thanks, I really am hungry."

She ate the pear.

Tom took out another rock and handed Anais a delicious piece of corn bread.

They walked all day, and as the night approached, they began to hear the sound of rushing water in the distance.

"We could walk a little farther but we better stop and wait to see where we are at dawn, unless you have a flashlight," Tom said jokingly.

"What's that?" Princess Anais asked.

"Oh, I was just kidding. Where I'm from, we have these things with batteries that light up so you can see in the dark."

Princess Anais smiled. "Oh, yes! What a good idea, Tom." And with that, the Magic Gown glowed so that the light led the way.

"Amazing!" said Tom.

By morning they had come upon the wide mouth of the Nojoke River. It was too wide and fast moving to cross. They would have been swept into the dark green waters by the strong current, so they hurried up along the riverbank and followed the river northerly.

It wasn't too long before Moregrott and his army of Lacks reached the riverbank. Not knowing which way Anais and Tom went, Moregrott pushed two of the Lacks into the river to swim across and see if

there was any sign of them. But they were quickly swept away and taken out to sea. Moregrott figured that Anais and Tom were headed up along the river and quickly started to pursue them.

Tom and Anais moved up along the Nojoke River. In the distance they could see the snow peaked Zumbrogarwan Mountain range.

"If we can get to those mountains, we have a better chance of hiding from Moregrott. Do you know where we are?" he asked Anais.

"I have been told stories of a land called the Wild Land of Skree, and farther north is the Land of Ker-Es, the land of the tenth king. I think that is where we must be headed," said Anais.

"I was told that the king has not been present for some time," she said, "and that those who live here are waiting for his return."

"Maybe he has returned," said Tom. "With his army, this king could stop Moregrott. We'll head to the mountains and find the tenth king."

As they approached the mountain range, they saw four huge snow-capped mountains like noble guards. They saw no trace of a tenth king or anyone else who lived there. In the distance farther north, they saw a sight they could not believe—a circle of seven majestic mountains glistening like jewels.

"Those are indeed the mountains of a king," Tom declared.

So they ran toward the Seven Jeweled Mountains of Ker-Es. They did not know that close behind them was a spying Lack, a fast Lack that Moregrott had sent up ahead to scout. The Lack heard them speak of the tenth king and jeweled mountains, and when he returned to Moregrott and told him what had been seen and what had been said, Moregrott shouted, "Ah, this plan is working out after all. I knew it!

There must be enormous treasure in those mountains where a king would live, and the Magic Gown will help me find it. If this tenth king has returned, I will kill him and make myself the ruler of this land. If he has not returned, then I will be the tenth king."

Tom and Anais continued to follow the river where it disappeared into the mountainside. Even though they were exhausted, they started to climb up between the mountains to get a better view of where the tenth king's palace might be. There was no sign of a palace or anyone. High up, in the center of the ring of the seven mountains, was a glistening lake. It was the Hidden Lake of Ker-Es. Princess Anais and Tom stood above the lake looking across the water. Princess Anais looked at Tom as he stared across the expanse of water and landscape. He looked radiant. She was suddenly struck with a thought, a memory. She was about to speak when, unexpectedly, they both smelled the horrible odor of Lacks and Tom felt his chest aching.

"I won't let Moregrott take you or the gown, Anais," Tom told her.

They turned to see Moregrott charging at them with his army. Tom and Anais ran down to the edge of the lake, but Moregrott caught Anais and grabbed her by the throat. Tom charged at Moregrott like a true protector but there were too many Lacks. They surrounded him. It became hard for him to breathe and he grew deathly pale. Moregrott's hands crippled with pain and he released Anais. She saw what was happening to Tom and turned and dove into the water. Moregrott and the Lacks immediately left Tom to go after her.

Tom called out weakly, almost completely drained of color, "No, Anais, don't."

Tom struggled to get up. He staggered to the water's edge and fell into the lake after her. He swam down deep but he could not find her. Underneath the shimmering glow of the water, he saw the gown floating and the oyster shell necklace falling silently to the bottom. There was no sign of Anais. Tom dove and caught the gown, but the necklace disappeared into deeper water beyond his grasp. A brilliant golden rainbow trout swam up to him and circled him. With no air left in his lungs, Tom had no choice but to swim to the surface, where he saw the

Lacks coming into the water after him. He saw them turn into flies one by one as the golden fish leaped from the water and began to eat every one of them. Tom swam to the shore holding the gown. The trout followed him to the riverbank.

It spoke to Tom. It was Anais's voice.

"Tom, you are the tenth king. I knew it when I saw you standing radiant on the mountain. Take the Magic Gown to the High Hibiscus Garden. You will understand all this then. You will know your destiny."

Tom was shocked.

"No, Anais," he said, "I'm not the tenth king. I'll go find him. You're wrong."

"You are the king," said the trout. "That is why the wind took The Lady Scarab to this land. Some things are certain and you are the tenth king. The wind knew. The Lady Scarab knew and the currents knew. They brought you to the Seven Jeweled Mountains and to the Hidden Lake of Ker-Es."

The brilliant-colored rainbow trout leaped in the air and dove deep down into the lake, leaving a splash and a swirl in the water.

Tom looked away from the water and saw Moregrott, gurgling and growling, and the army of Lacks that had not been turned into flies running at him and the Magic Gown. He turned once more to look in the water for the trout, but she was not there. He ran. He ran in search of the tenth king. All he could see was the circle of seven shimmering jeweled mountains surrounding the Hidden Lake of Ker-es. All he knew was that the Lacks were close behind and getting closer.

CHAPTER 9

Through The Pass

The Butterfly Cliffs towered straight up from the ground, colored in the brightest red and yellow. Through the center of the cliffs was a pass. It was pouring down raining and Lilly used Cameo's staff to help her climb the steep slippery rock and dirt to the pass. The wind blew hard off the cliff tops, making an eerie musical sound. This was a strange place. The stone cliff walls seemed to move, as if they were covered with thousands of red and yellow butterflies.

"My eyes are playing tricks on me," Lilly said to herself.

Through the opening, Lilly could see in the distance a large brown rock and then the forest.

If I could just run to that rock, she thought.

Lilly began to run toward the opening but stumbled and fell into the wet dirt in the middle of the pass between the sheer cliff walls. Flat on her back looking up at the rock walls on either side of her, she saw the walls moving. She rolled onto her stomach, and with the big rock in her sight, she got to her feet and ran as fast as she could. Once at the rock, she turned around in time to see the cliffs disappearing into the air as hundreds of thousands of glittering red and yellow butterflies

flew swirling and spiraling upwards. The cliffs were no longer there. Lilly sat down on the rock, panting to catch her breath.

"Hey! Who's that?" Lilly heard from beneath her.

Lilly jumped to her feet and looked at the rock that had just spoken to her.

"Did you say something, rock?"

The rock gave a big yawn. "Yes."

"Oh, I'm sorry," Lilly said. "I didn't notice."

"Hmmm, yes, well, this is the Sleeping Forest. We've all been asleep here. We're waiting. Even the trees are asleep. If you listen you can hear them snoring."

"Waiting for what?" she asked.

"I don't remember exactly," he said sleepily.

"Who are you and where did you come from?" asked the rock.

"I'm Lilly and I came through the pass of the Butterfly Cliffs, but they just disappeared."

Lilly turned and saw that the red and yellow Butterfly Cliffs were back in place, as if they had never disappeared.

"Well, anyway, I came from the High Hibiscus Garden, and I am looking for the cedar stump."

"Oh! Well, nice to meet you, miss," the rock said. "Thanks for waking me up."

"How long have you been sleeping?" Lilly asked.

"I don't remember, but it must have been a long time because I'm feeling very hungry," he answered and made a chomping sound.

Lilly stepped back.

"A cup of tea would be lovely, and toast with butter and honey," he said.

Lilly came closer again and reached for the pouch around her neck. "Here, I have some Springtree honey!"

She poured a little bit of honey into the rocks mouth.

"Thank you, delicious!" he said, suddenly glowing with a new bright copper color. Lilly gave him another taste and he licked his lips.

"Hmmm, now let's see; ah yes, the cedar stump is in the forest somewhere. That I remember. I've heard the chipzies talk about that place. It's the fairies favorite spot."

"Chipzies? What're chipzies?"

"Shy little ones, pine nut farmers. I don't know if they're here in the forest anymore. If they are, they can take you to the cedar stump. Now pardon me for askin', miss, but why do you need to find the cedar stump?"

Lilly bent close to the rock and said, "King Cameo, the ninth king—this is his staff—he told me to find the cedar stump; there I will find my direction. I'm on an important mission, rock, a magical one. A kind of secret."

"Oh really? And you've been to the High Hibiscus Garden and seen them? The star travelers?"

"Oh yes."

"So it's true! It's all true what Nizella has told me."

"Nizella? Who's that?"

"The rarest of fairies."

Lilly wanted to keep talking to the rock. Talking about fairies was her favorite thing to do, and the rock was good company. She wanted to hear all about Nizella and the chipzies, but she needed to be on her way. Now the thought of entering a sleeping forest by herself made her feel a little jumpy.

"Rock, I should be going. I'd ask you to come but . . ."

"I know, but I'm a rock, kinda slow to travel with. That's okay, miss. You best be on your way."

"Yeah, thanks for the good company," she said, as she tasted some honey and gave him a little more before closing the pouch.

"Oh, okay, miss. It's been nice meetin' ya."

"Bye, rock," she waved. "Wish me luck."

"Good luck is already yours, Lilly," he said and began to whistle a happy tune.

Lilly walked carefully past the huge sleeping pine, oak, maple and locust trees. This was an ancient forest. She heard the trees softly snoring. Every once in a while she heard some leaves rustling and some yawns. Apart from the noise of the sleeping trees, the forest was dead quiet: no birds, no insects, just slumbering trees and Lilly's footsteps. Walking near a thick bed of dried pine needles, Lilly tripped on something soft and stumbled and fell. Something in the pine needles felt lumpy. She felt around. Brushing the needles away, Lilly discovered five little sleeping creatures, all together in an intertwined group. They looked like tiny chipmunk people. They were about a foot tall and wore different bright-colored woolen coats and pants and brown leather boots. Lilly giggled at the sight of the sleepy creatures. Chipmunks always made her smile no matter what the situation. *These must be the chipzies*, she thought. She shook one of the little creatures.

"Hello, hello. Wake up."

The large pine above her snored and stretched, and several pinecones fell from its branches, falling onto her and the chipmunk people.

One of them, with a little green hat, yellow coat and black pants, opened its eyes.

"What's going on . . . ? Oh! A fairy! Look!" he called out to the others. "Monk, Sandy, Robin, Red, a fairy has returned! A big fairy!"

Another chipzy, dressed in a blue jacket and brown pants, sat up. "What is it, Tic? Fairies? Fairies!" He jumped up.

"Hi. I'm not a fairy. I'm Lilly."

"What's a Lilly?" Monk asked.

"No, I'm Lilly, a girl, and who are you?"

"A girl? What's a girl?" Tic said, looking behind her. "Where are your wings? Can you not fly?"

"Sandy, wake up. The fairy lost her wings!" Monk pushed Sandy, who wore a bright pink coat and tan pants.

"I don't have wings. I'm not a fairy. I'm a girl."

Now all five of the chipzies stood up, looking at Lilly, looking at her back for the missing wings.

"The rock said you know where the cedar stump is. I need to find it as soon as possible," said Lilly, trying to get their attention.

"You're not a fairy and you want us to show you where the cedar stump is . . . the enchanted cedar stump?" Red commented suspiciously. "Ah, I don't know about that. These are cautious times indeed."

"Now, Red, don't be like that. These are magical times indeed," Tic insisted, pointing to the two feathers in her hair.

"And look, Red, the Lilly is carrying Cameo's staff," Monk said, admiring the beautiful spiraled white, gold and silver wooden staff.

"True! Impressive for sure!" remarked Red. "And convincing . . . okay, magical times it is, but I remain cautious. Now let's eat."

"Breakfast first!" Sandy called out.

"Where is it, where is it?" asked Robin, who wore an orange jacket and short brown pants and pushed away the dried pine needles looking for something.

"Here it is!" Tic held up a small colorful wooden guitar and gave it to Robin.

"Oh, thank goodness!" cried Robin. "The fairies love music."

"We don't know if the fairies have returned, Rob. Don't get your hopes up," Red commented.

"Today is auspicious and I am ever hopeful," Robin declared merrily and strummed the strings of the little wooden guitar.

After they all had a generous helping of pine nuts and Springtree honey, the chipzies and Lilly headed for the center of the forest. The forest now seemed to be waking up. Trees yawned and stretched as they passed by. Robin's music brought little creatures out of tree holes and underground dens, rubbing their eyes and scratching their heads.

"No sign of fairies, Tic," Red commented.

"Well, we won't know for certain until we find the cedar stump, Red."

"What if it's not there, Tic," Red said, slipping back into pessimism. "Maybe it was stolen or . . ."

"Shhh . . . enough!" Monk told Red.

"Or what?" asked Lilly.

"Red's just being nervous and worried because . . ."

"Because he is in love with the fairy Nizella, and she disappeared with all the fairies," added Monk.

"Be quiet, Monk," said Red, as he blushed deeply.

"Please tell me. Why did the fairies disappear?" asked Lilly.

"We don't know. They just vanished one day, and then the forest fell into a deep sleep like a drowsy spell. Something happened, some change. We never knew what it was. The fairies knew though."

"Oh," said Lilly. "I wonder if it had anything to do with the Magic Gown."

The five chipzies stopped and looked at each other.

"The Magic Gown that Princess Anais wears?" Tic asked.

"Yes, I'm supposed to find her and the Magic Gown. That's where I am going. The cedar stump will help me find the right direction."

Red spoke, "Oh, this is good news. Come on, come on!"

It seemed like two days went by as they walked through the forest and finally rested when they came to a clearing. A pale yellow-green light shone through the trees onto a venerable old cedar stump. The chipzies looked around and called out, "Nizella, are you here?" But all was quiet and there was no sign of fairies.

Lilly noticed the stump was leaning in a certain direction.

"Which way is that pointing?" Lilly asked.

"The in-between land, the Canyonlands. None of us have ever been there before. It is a pale-colored place where the magic is so strong it's tricky. It lies before the Wild Land of Skree and the unknown city and the Hidden Lake of Ker-Es farther north."

"That's the way I should go. I know it. And I have to go alone. Well, me and the staff."

"Oh, are you sure?" said Tic, "We've never been out of the forest but we'd go with you."

"I'm sure, but you wait here for the fairies. When they come, you'll know I've found Princess Anais and the Magic Gown."

"Please be careful!" said Sandy.

The chipzies decided to wait by the cedar stump. They hoped the fairies would be returning soon, now that the forest was waking up. They would collect more pine nuts. They thanked Lilly for the Springtree honey and said goodbye to her.

Lilly hurried along a path lined by very tall pine trees. She felt lively and invigorated; her feet were gliding swiftly over the pine needles, barely grazing the ground. Maybe it was the strong magic. Maybe it was the end of her quest. At the end of the waking-up Sleeping Forest, she came to the beginning of the Canyonlands. She walked swiftly and saw nothing but scrub pines, low bushes of tiny yellow flowers and an occasional bee that she pretended came all the way from the Springtree.

The night in the Canyonlands was windy. The starlight was like nothing she had ever seen. Spectacular stars lit the sky and kept her and the staff company. The morning light revealed a dry riverbed that led uphill in one of the canyons, so she followed it. As she continued farther into the canyon, she suddenly felt "butterflies" in her stomach. She looked for Theresa, but the butterfly wasn't there.

CHAPTER 10

The Magic Gown

Tom scrambled down the side of the mountain. He moved quickly toward a steep gully and jumped in. Running down the center, he slid along as rocks and dirt slid with him like an avalanche. It wasn't long before he heard Moregrott's voice. "You can't hide from me, boy!" Tom looked up and saw Moregrott and his army lining the top of the gully. He kept moving as fast as his feet could carry him. Behind him, crazed Lacks were charging down the gully, gaining on him as Moregrott watched from above. Tom stumbled and fell. Eerily, the wind stirred past him. Suddenly, a bright red, blue, green and yellow swirl swooped by him, pulling strongly at the gown. He heard windy voices, "swoooowh", sounded the wind, "swoooowh." It pulled at the dress again. Tom let the colorful wind sweep the gown away just as the Lacks caught up to him. The gown flew high into the air where no Lack could reach it.

Moregrott scowled and screamed as he came pouncing down the gully toward them, "Follow that gown!"

Tom's heart ached unbearably. He gasped for air and grew pale. Being near the Lacks without the protection of the Magic Gown was deadly.

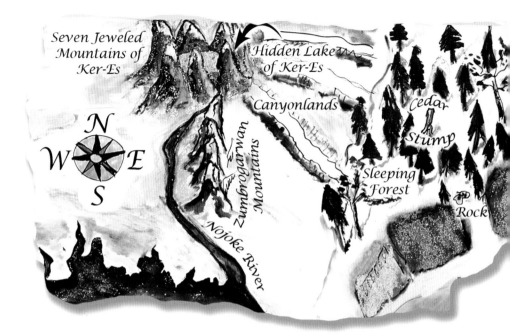

The gown flew high over the Canyonlands until it slowly drifted down into the dry riverbed that Lilly was, at that moment, walking up. The Lacks raced toward the canyon and the gown.

Lilly paused and stood holding the staff. She did not hear Moregrott but felt his presence. Her heart began to ache and then she smelled the horrible stench of Lacks. "Oh, no!" She began to run up the dry riverbed, jumping over rocks and fallen logs. Up ahead she saw a circle of stones on the riverbed floor. There, lying in the stone circle, was a torn and weathered old dress. *What is that?* she thought.

"Stay away from it!" yelled an ugly, scrawny Lack who was charging toward her.

"That is Moregrott's, not yours!" it gurgled.

She hurried toward the dress, but before she could get to it, the Lack jumped on her, knocking the staff from her hand. In seconds, her color was draining away. She struggled to fight off the putrid smelling Lack. In her struggle, she didn't notice the staff changing, as the head of a smiling serpent, with big orange and blue eyes, emerged from the wood. Another Lack jumped onto Lilly, and her heart ached so bad she began to cry white tears. The more she cried, the louder the two Lacks gurgled. Her tears ran down her face onto the ground, like a tiny stream of milk, and touched the staff. The staff wiggled. Its dark green head and bright orange and blue eyes lifted off the ground. Like a giant snake, it moved toward the attacking monsters. It coiled up and lashed at them, hissing and speaking in a voice that Lilly would never forget.

"I am the Staff of the Ninth King. Beware of my bite!"

The two creatures snarled and gurgled at the snake and tried to drain the life from it with their empty vacuum eyes. But the snake's colors only brightened as it coiled back, leaped at one of the Lacks and bit into its leg. The Lack whined in pain and moved from Lilly. The snake leaped at the other Lack and sank his teeth into its arm. It screeched and dropped to the ground, releasing Lilly. She struggled to her feet and made it to where the gown was lying. She picked it up and held it close to her body. More Lacks coming down the canyon charged toward her. The glowing snake hissed, striking at them. A huge Lack got by and grabbed Lilly by the arm. Surprisingly, the Lack fell to the ground writhing, calling out, "No! No, not me!" Then, with several loud shrieks, it shrank to a small worm creature. Light blue luminescent wings popped out from its sides and the worm turned into a sapphire blue dragonfly. More Lacks came near Lilly, like she was some kind of magnet, and touched her. As they did, they, too, turned into brilliant blue, green, orange, gold or purple dragonflies.

Soon the dragonflies swirled around her like pieces of flying light. Lilly slipped the dress over her head, but instead of being torn and old, the Magic Gown was whole and glowing.

Moregrott, coming down the riverbed and seeing what was happening, screamed, "Stay away from her! Don't touch her!"

Lilly turned to see Moregrott. "Where is Princess Anais?" she demanded.

He gave a hideous laugh, exclaiming, "Drowned in the lake! Sacrificed herself for nothing! Never to be seen again! Gone!" as he lifted Anais's crown in the air as proof of her death.

"And I'm not done with you or that stupid boy!"

What boy? Lilly thought.

Lilly saw the rest of the Lacks coming down from the canyon carrying a very pale boy who was very obviously a human. Lilly could not believe her eyes. It looked for all the world just like the boy in the photograph at the Finch's house. It looked like Tom Finch!

"Give me the gown and I will give you him, or he will surely die."

Moregrott grabbed Tom's limp body. Lilly moved toward them but Moregrott, holding Tom, backed away, not wanting to be touched by her.

"I beg you to let him go. Please, Moregrott," Lilly pleaded.

Moregrott growled, "He will die soon. Give me the gown."

Lilly could not let Tom die. She started to take off the dress. The snake quietly crawled closer to Moregrott's foot. Just as Lilly was about to pull the dress over her head, the snake coiled and struck. It bit deep

into Moregrott's foot and he squealed in pain and stumbled backwards, dropping Tom onto the ground. Lilly slipped the gown back down and ran to him. Moregrott reached for Lilly in a dazed fury. His dirty long nails and fingers clasped around her ankle. Still in pain, Moregrott sneered and mocked her.

"See, a stupid little girl like you has no power over me even with the gown on. Give it to me or you will both die." He clutched onto her arm and pulled at the gown.

He screamed crazily, his hands cramping. "Stop that! No!" he yelled at someone or something. "No, not me! Help!"

The gown glowed shimmering colors of yellow, pink, green, lavender and blue.

Moregrott's mottled light gray skin began turning to a pale orange. All of a sudden he lay motionless. He seemed dead.

Lilly stared at the still creature lying near her and knelt down next to the boy.

"Hello, Hello," Lilly said quietly to the boy, as she tried to pull him away from Moregrott. "Tom?"

Moregrott stirred and moaned. Lilly tried to pull Tom farther away. Moregrott's skin began to grow orange and black fur. His hands curled and softened. He rolled onto his back, rolling from side to side, crying and sobbing.

Lilly saw fur, ears, paws. Moregrott was now a huge tiger. Its bright yellow eyes snapped opened and looked at Lilly. It leaped to its feet in a frenzy, jumping toward her just inches from her face and growling. Lacks came charging at her and at the lifeless Tom. The tiger roared. Lilly squeezed her eyes shut and held her breath. She stood still, expecting him to pounce on her, but instead, the tiger began devouring the Lacks one by one until they were all gone. He turned and looked at Lilly. He stood for a moment, his gaze locked into hers, and then ran up the canyon, disappearing from sight.

Lilly sat down next to the boy, who was barely breathing, and gently touched his chest, then his face and whispered, "Tom?"

His eyes were closed and there was no response. She slipped the honey pouch from over her head and opened it, letting drops of honey get onto his lips and into his mouth. 'Tom," she called again. A little color returned to his face. He opened his eyes. She smiled at him. He tasted the honey on his lips. He lifted his hand and touched her face and then the shell around her neck.

"You're wearing the gown. Who are you?" he asked.

"Lilly," she responded.

"Lilly," he repeated.

"You're Tom Finch, aren't you?"

"Yes, I am. How do you know?"

"I'm from your world. I know your parents and Jake, your dog."
Some more color returned to his face.

"Where's Princess Anais?" Lilly asked. "Were you with her?"

"I was with her but she is now in the lake. She saved me. I was supposed to save her." Tom slowly got up looking around. "Where is he? Where are Moregrott and the Lacks?" Lilly pointed to the shimmering dragonflies that flew around them. "Those are some of the Lacks and Moregrott turned into a huge tiger and ate the rest, but he left us alone. This really is a magic gown."

He walked over to the staff lying in the riverbed and picked it up.

"That's King Cameo's staff, Princess Anais's father, from the High Hibiscus Garden," said Lilly.

"Oh! Her father? I feel so terrible about what happened. I must go to him, to the High Hibiscus Garden." Tom held his head, still dizzy and overcome by the loss of Princess Anais.

"Is that where you're from?" he asked.

"No," said Lilly, "I told you, I'm from your world."

"Oh, yeah. How did you get here?"

"It's unbelievable how I got here," she told him.

"Oh, I think I might believe it," he replied.

Lilly saw Princess Anais's crown lying near a rock and walked over to it, kneeled down and picked it up.

"I was supposed to help her too, Tom," she said sadly.

They were silent.

"I wish I could have met her again," said Lilly.

"You met her before?" asked Tom.

"Yes, a long time ago," said Lilly. "Let's go, Tom, to look for her."

"We can go, Lilly, but Princess Anais is a fish now and who knows if we can find her."

"A fish? Tom, let's go and see. I need to try."

They climbed high into the mountains to reach the Hidden Lake of Ker-Es. As they stood on the edge of the lake, looking to see if

Princess Anais would appear, they saw their reflection in the water. Suddenly, beside them, the image of a huge tiger face appeared. Tom and Lilly held hands tightly and held their breath. They could hear the tiger's deep growling as he inched closer. They stood still and looked into the tiger's yellow eyes reflected in the water.

"It's Moregrott," Lilly whispered under her breath to Tom.

"Hello, Moregrott. How have you been?" Tom said, breaking the silent tension.

The tiger stopped growling.

"I have not been well, thank you for asking."

It didn't sound like the monster Moregrott anymore.

"I am sad and very sorry for all that I have done," the tiger said.

"I no longer want to be called Moregrott. I have to think of a new name. Can you think of any that suit me?" the tiger asked.

Tom looked into the tiger's soulful eyes. "Hmm . . ."

"How about Viktor? What do you think about that, Lilly?" Tom asked.

"Yes, I like Viktor very much," said Lilly. "It suits you."

"Viktor, yes," the tiger said and rubbed his head affectionately against Tom. Tom stroked his strong neck and felt a big old scar.

"I remember this one," said Tom. It was the wound Tom had made on Moregrott's neck when he stabbed him with the jagged piece of wood on The Lady Scarab.

"Sorry about that, Viktor."

"That's okay, Tom."

"I wish I could say I was sorry to Princess Anais," Viktor said.

"Me too," said Lilly.

"Me too," added Tom.

Together, the three stood at the edge of the lake sur-rounded by the seven moun-tains. Viktor spoke, looking out onto the lake.

"When I touched the Magic Gown in the canyon, I heard a beautiful voice speaking to me."

"Yes, I heard it too," said Lilly.

"I did not understand what was happening. I turned into a tiger and devoured the Lacks who were trying to hurt you. I came to this lake to look for Princess Anais."

As Viktor told Tom and Lilly his story, big tears began to run down his face like pearls and dripped off his long whiskers into the lake.

"Look where I came from," he reflected: "the bones of greedy people. How could I be good? I had poisoned myself thinking that Moregrott was all that I was, so lost and hateful. I hurt people and other living things. It's not right to do that! I didn't know there was anything good in me."

Lilly stroked his head.

Without their noticing, far out in the center of the lake the golden rainbow trout leaped out of the water and a swirl of bright colors rose into the air. Then the fish dove back into the water, making a splashing sound that echoed around the Seven Jeweled Mountains. They heard it and looked to see what it was, but only the circles of ripples in the water were visible.

The tiger continued, "As I stood right here and looked at my new reflection in the lake, I began to feel a strength in me, a strength I never knew I had, and I felt kindness come over me."

Lilly walked into the shallow water and bent down closer to the water's surface. Drifting toward the edge in the ripples of the water was a golden yellow rose. Lilly picked it out of the water and said, "I believe this is for you, Viktor, from Anais."

The three of them looked out over the water for any evidence of Princess Anais, but the water was now quiet and still.

"I am going to stay here with Princess Anais," said Viktor.

"Yes, and be her guardian and the guardian of the Hidden Lake of Ker-Es!" declared Tom.

Viktor lay down by the lake's edge, looking so peaceful and majestic.

Tom and Lilly left Viktor by the lakeside and began to walk down toward the canyon as Lilly told Tom her story. She told him how she had met his parents, and he told her how he had followed the silver current one morning and come to the Great Desert.

"How long do you think we've been gone?" he asked her.

"Well, you disappeared in the summer and have been gone for a while. It was the end of December when I went through the doorway to the Great Desert of Uncertainty," explained Lilly.

"Amazing, Lilly, simply amazing! But in a way, I'm not surprised; wild stuff has been happening to me all my life," he explained.

"It seems so," Lilly affirmed.

They followed the riverbed down to the Sleeping Forest and found the enchanted cedar stump. A green-yellow glowing light beamed down on it. On top of the stump sat the beautiful fairy queen Nizella nibbling on some pine nuts. It was the very fairy that Lilly met in the forest, the one who helped her and Ming Li.

"It is good to see the tenth king has arrived. We have been waiting for you for quite a long time. I am Nizella, and the fairy kingdom welcomes you, King Tom, to the Forest of Ker-Es. And welcome to you, Lilly. I see you are wearing the Magic Gown."

Lilly looked at Tom and exclaimed, "Tom, you're the tenth king!"

Tom shrugged his shoulders. "No! How could that be? That's ridiculous and impossible. I'm from the other world like you, Lilly."

She walked closer to him and took his hands.

"Tom, think about it; you could be. No one knows who your parents were or where you came from. You were miraculously found in the mountains. It sounds like a king's tale to me. I think you are a star traveler."

"A what? No, I'm not the tenth king! I just followed the silver current and ended up here with you. Who knows why?"

"To follow the silver current was your destiny. It has always been," Nizella told him.

As Nizella spoke to Tom, a memory flashed before Lilly. Nizella stopped talking and looked at Lilly. "What is it you want to ask me, Lilly?"

"Merciles said she killed Ming Li; is she okay?" asked Lilly.

"Merciles's Lacks tried but did not succeed. Ming Li recovered and flew off, saying she had something very important to do."

"Thank you for helping her," Lilly said and kissed Nizella.

The fairy queen smiled.

"I see you found the Springtree," said the fairy queen, pointing to the honey pouch.

Bright colored winged fairies and the five chipzies appeared from out of the forest and circled the enchanted cedar stump.

"The forest is awake again," Tic declared. Robin cheerfully played his little wooden guitar.

Red was delighted to see Nizella after all this time.

The music played and floated far into the Canyonlands and up to the Hidden Lake of Ker-Es. Pine nuts were passed around, and Lilly shared the Springtree honey with everyone there to celebrate the forest waking up and the arrival of Tom, the tenth king, even though he really didn't believe it.

CHAPTER **11**

Returning Home

Tom and Lilly said goodbye to Nizella, the chipzies, and the fairies of the forest, and to the rock, when they passed it while on their way to the Butterfly Cliffs. In time they reached the familiar path and entered the High Hibiscus Garden. Once again, two majestic eagles sat high up in the branches. They glided down and landed softly in front of Lilly and Tom, transforming once more into the woman-bird, White Tears, and the man-bird, Cameo.

Lilly slipped the gown off over her head and extended it to White Tears.

"I was supposed to help Anais," Lilly said. "Please take the gown back. I have failed."

Tom stepped forward holding Princess Anais's crown and Cameo's staff.

"It is I who have failed. She saved me from my own death and protected the Magic Gown by becoming a fish in the lake. I am so sorry."

White Tears took the crown from Tom's hand and held it close to her face, whispering something in the strange language. The crown began to glow with tiny flames. The emeralds and amber jewels shimmered and glistened as they seemed to be moving and then, suddenly, turned into green and golden hummingbirds that flew around them.

"Your twin sister's spirit is even stronger than before, my dear son," White Tears said to him.

Tom looked stunned and dropped to his knees. Cameo and White Tears came to him and helped him stand. Cameo picked up his staff.

"We have been waiting for you to return to the Land. We knew when you were ready, you would return," Cameo said, tearfully embracing his son.

"What do you mean?" asked Tom.

"We knew you would return when it was time for the Magic Gown to go to the other world, that you would come back to us as the Magic Gown departed," his mother explained, kissing his face so happy to see him.

The hummingbirds were circling Lilly. Then they began to circle Tom. Then they flew to the edge of the garden, circling faster and faster into a shimmering spiral of greens and gold. As Tom and Lilly looked into the center of the spiral, something seemed to be developing. A figure slowly appeared. It was Princess Anais, walking through the fluttering hummingbirds as if she had never been a fish. The birds settled on her head and changed back into the amber and emerald jewels in the fruitwood crown she wore. Lilly ran to her. The princess held out the shell necklace she wore, the necklace like Lilly wore.

"Hello, Lilly. It is so good to see you again."

"Hello!" Lilly beamed with delight and they embraced.

Tom came close and took Anais's hand.

"My sister, thank you."

"You're welcome, my brother," she said, and kissed his cheek. "Thank you for getting the Magic Gown to Lilly."

She ran to her parents, who embraced her tightly.

White Tears spoke to Lilly.

"The Magic Gown is yours now, Lilly," she continued. "Take it to your world. Do with it as your heart instructs you. You will know."

"Wonderful, wonderful magic," Princess Anais whispered to her, and the two girls laughed and hugged.

"Son, you are the tenth king, the King of the Land of Ker-Es. You have spent necessary time in the other world. You learned its ways and returned here when the silver current of the crescent moon appeared to you. You walked in the Great Desert of Uncertainty and met face to face the creature Moregrott and brought the gown to Lilly with the help of your sister and the Colorful Wind."

"Moregrott is now Viktor, the tiger king, Father," Tom said and told him how Moregrott touched the Magic Gown. "He has been transformed: majestic, wise and caring."

"All is as it should be," said White Tears as she turned to Lilly.

"The Lady Scarab is waiting for you at Honeybee Cove. She will sail you through the silver mist past the Great Desert of Uncertainty, and from there you will find your way back. It has been arranged."

"Rest here tonight and tomorrow you will leave," said Cameo.

"I will take Lilly," said Tom.

The next morning, Lilly and Tom climbed down the Rubyrock Falls. At the bottom, Rue and Mik waited to escort them through the mist of the Red Tree Forest, where the magic remained very, very strong. Tall red trees towered around them. At the beginning of the Deep Blue River, where the first blue tree appeared, Zara stood waiting for them.

Lilly ran to her, delighted to finally see her again after she had told her to go away in the kitchen.

"You were right, Zara," Lilly exclaimed. "Magic is all around me. Thank you, thank you for visiting me that day."

"You're welcome. The time of goodness has truly come!"

Tom approached Zara.

"Hello, I'm Tom Finch."

"Yes, I know."

Just then they heard singing and colorful flowers began to fall gently from the sky, landing in their hair and all around them. Walking toward them along the Deep Blue River was Joseph, the elephant.

"It is good to see you again, young Tom. Let me take a good look at you. My, how you have grown," he said.

"Have we met before?" asked Tom.

"Oh yes, I cared for you in the mountains years ago."

"That was you? You were the mountain man, Joseph?" Tom asked, as his eyes filled with tears of joy. Lilly and Tom saw the elephant transform before them into the mountain man. He had deep violet-blue eyes, mahogany brown skin and long silver hair. He wore a long blue coat with silver and blue turquoise buttons.

"Yes, I was and I am. We went together to the singing mountain far to the north to a special place. It was our destiny together," Joseph said.

"Thank you," Tom said and hugged him, touched by the love he felt for Joseph.

Rue, Mik, Zara, Joseph, Lilly and Tom came to the cove where The Lady Scarab was waiting for them. The wind billowed in the bright yellow sails of the lovely wooden ship. Lilly and Tom boarded the vessel and sailed away from the shoreline of Honeybee Cove heading south across the silver water. Nearing the coast of the Great Desert of Uncertainty, they saw the giant purple flying dragon standing tall at the shore waving to them.

"Hello, Silly Lilly," he called, and the wind carried his voice.

"Hello, Mr. H. Myrrh! Hello, Mr. Hugh Myrrh! Thank you for everything," Lilly called back.

The Lady Scarab sailed past the Great Desert and approached the silver mist. Tom dropped the sails. Silently the ship coasted into the mist. CLUNK! There, sitting in the water, was the Star-Gazer. "My boat! I wondered where it went. It's waiting here for you, Lilly, to take you and the Magic Gown home."

Tom threw a rope onto the boat. "I suppose I could go back with you and see my parents . . ." He was quiet. "But this is where I belong now. Will you tell them about me, Lilly, if you can?"

Lilly shrugged her shoulders and said, "I'll try but I don't think anyone will believe me."

"I want to stay here with you," said Lilly, as tears rolled down her cheeks.

"I would love that, Lilly, but you have the Magic Gown to take back. Maybe the magic will bring you back sometime."

She embraced him.

His eyes filled with tears.

Tom helped Lilly climb down onto the Star-Gazer. "She'll take good care of you."

He leaned way over the side toward Lilly and kissed her. The boats parted and the Star-Gazer drifted farther into the silver mist. Lilly watched Tom standing on the deck of The Lady Scarab as they disappeared from her sight. From out of the mist, she heard Tom's voice call her name.

"Lilly, thank you!"

"Tom," she cried out and listened, but she heard nothing.

A small figure flew toward her in the mist. It was Ming Li.

"Hello, Ming Li! I'm so glad you came to say goodbye. I don't want to leave."

The white moth fluttered by her and Lilly couldn't believe her eyes when, from behind Ming Li, she saw J. The blue jay rested on the side of the Star-Gazer and squawked at Lilly.

"J," Lilly shouted, "you're alive!"

She looked at Ming Li.

"He was dead," she said. "How is this possible?"

"It seems the dragon's gold rock you threw down Merciles's throat did some magic and brought J back to life. J flew from the wicked witch's throat and escaped onto the lavender tundra. He followed you and found his way to the Springtree, to Stee-Ven, who found me."

"That's so great," Lilly cried. "I'm gonna miss it here. I'm gonna miss everyone and the magic."

"Dear Lilly, you are taking the magic with you."

Ming Li fluttered nearer to her and kissed Lilly's cheek.

"Look for us in your dreams."

The moth flew back into the silver mist.

"Goodbye, Ming Li, thank you," Lilly called.

The boat drifted deeper into the mist.

"I'm so glad your here, J."

The silvery fog thinned and disappeared completely. It was daylight and snow was falling. She turned the key and tried the engine. It started. She motored through the inlet and down the river, coming up to Tom's house. Extra-large snowflakes began to fall. Within seconds, Lilly and J were in a heavy snowstorm and couldn't see anything around them. The Star-Gazer kept going as if on auto-pilot. She thought they were passing by Mrs. London's house when she smelled scones baking.

"Mmmm, they smell good, don't they, J?"

The little boat slowed and drifted to the edge of the creek near the woods. Lilly climbed over the side and stood on the deep snow covered ground. Lilly walked through the woods and soon could see her house in the clearing and smell the wood fire burning in the fireplace. She ran up to the house and opened the door. Her father was at the piano.

"Hi, Daddy!"

He looked up.

"Lilly! What were you doing outside in this blizzard without a coat and what do you have there?"

Lilly ran to him and put her arms around him.

"Where's Mommy?"

"Lilly!"

Her mother called from the basement. Katherine came up the basement stairs.

"You weren't down there, where were you? I thought I had heard something!"

Lilly's mother was holding a small gold rock.

"What's that?" Lilly pointed to the rock.

"I don't know. It was on the stairs. What's that?"

She pointed to the dress Lilly was holding.

Lilly looked down at the old ripped dress, puzzled.

"I don't know. I don't know where I got it. I was out in the snow with J but . . ."

"But you forgot your jacket, Lil. Are you okay?"

Her mom felt her forehead and looked at Andrew in a nervous panic.

"Oh dear! What's happening? Is it happening again?"

"Is what happening?" Lilly questioned. She felt around her neck. She was wearing the shell necklace. Her fingers felt something else. Lilly pulled at a string around her neck, and from under her clothes she uncovered the small pouch.

"Where'd this come from?" she asked her parents.

"I don't know, you tell us," her mother said nervously. "Did you make it?"

"No!" Lilly answered, close to tears.

"Well, you're full of surprises today, Lil," Andrew consoled her.

"Maybe the Finches gave it to you?" he suggested, noticing the feathers in her hair.

Lilly began to cry.

Her mother felt the pouch.

Lilly pulled away.

She ran to get her jacket off the hook and slipped it on as she closed the door behind her.

"Lilly!" her mother called out the door.

Lilly ran out through the woods to the creek, where she stood to see if anything made sense to her, but there was nothing there. There were no clues. She couldn't remember.

All was quiet. The snow fell.

She went back to the house. Her mother met her at the door and said, "Is everything okay?"

Lilly yawned as she took off her coat. "I'm so sleepy! I just need to . . . ," she gave another big yawn.

"Go on upstairs, sweetheart, and take a nap before dinner."

Lilly went up the stairs to her room and sat on the bed. She fell fast asleep holding the ripped gown.

"Lilly, wake up. I have dinner for you," her mother said gently as she stood by her bed.

"Let her sleep. She'll feel better in the morning. I'll check on her in a little while," said her dad.

The next morning, Lilly awoke to a clear, sunny winter day. The snow crystals glistened and shimmered. Lilly found the gown crumpled under her covers.

She sighed. "You're still here."

She slipped it on over her head. Looking in the mirror, Lilly discovered that it was no longer ripped.

"What! That's impossible."

As if to answer her, the dress glowed with colors.

"Hello, Lilly!" She heard a deep voice coming from outside her window. She ran to the window and saw a large white seagull with a bright orange and gold fish in its mouth sitting on the snowy blue spruce branch.

She slid the window up.

"Hey!" she called. "I know you. You're Tu and The Fish and . . ."

"And you'll never forget again, Lilly," The Fish called to her.

Tu lifted off the branch and flew toward her, landing on the windowsill.

The Fish spoke.

"The magic is here now, Lilly. The Colorful Wind will soon come and then the star travelers!"

"They will? When?" she asked.

"Watch the roses, plant them in the spring," The Fish instructed her.

There was a knock at her bedroom door.

"Lilly?" her mother called.

The door opened.

Tu, with The Fish in his mouth, flew from the windowsill.

Her mother stood in the doorway. "Good morning! How ya feeling, Lil? Breakfast is ready. You must be . . ." Her mother suddenly stopped speaking, noticing the glowing gown.

Lilly looked down at the dress and smiled.

"It's the Magic Gown. I remember everything now. I brought it back from the Land of Ten Kings and Roses and . . ."

"Lilly, you better take that off. Please stop talking like that," her mother insisted, her eyes fixed firmly on the dress.

"But it is the Magic Gown, Mommy."

"Don't start this. I'm calling the doctor."

"I don't need a doctor. I feel great."

The gown glowed brighter. Colors danced around it. Katherine sat on the edge of the bed captivated. Lilly noticed two gold rocks in her mother's hands.

"That's Mik's gold rock from Mr. H. Myrrh. Why do you have two of them? Wasn't there only one in the basement?"

Katherine hesitated.

"Yes, there was."

"But you have two."

Once again, her mother hesitated.

". . . My grandmother gave me this one when I was a little girl. She told me she had been given it from a very special place."

"It is! It's dragon's gold from the Great Desert of Uncertainty in the Land of Ten Kings and Roses."

"The Land of Ten Kings and Roses?" Katherine repeated.

"Yeah, that's where I went when I was a little girl by the waterfall in Brazil. The hummingbirds took me. And that's where I was yesterday . . ."

"Oh! How did you know about that, I never told. . . ?"

Her mother stopped talking and drifted into thought.

"What, Mommy? What is it?"

"Grandma's stories," she replied, bewildered.

Lilly walked closer to her mother.

"What about my great-grandma?"

"She told me stories about these places. I thought she was just silly and old."

"No. She is a star traveler like you and me. The star travelers are coming . . . Oh! I have to tell the Finches about Tom," she said, slipping the gown off over her head and laying it on the bed. "I have to tell them I was with him and that he is okay."

"Lilly, what are you talking about?"

"You just can't go to the Finches' and say that. It sounds awful crazy."

"See, there you go again, not believing! They knew Tom was special. They'll believe me." Lilly began to dress swiftly.

Katherine cautiously picked up the gown.

Lilly went to leave the room. "I have to go to the Finches'."

"Lilly, wait!" her mother called.

Lilly turned. The gown was glowing in her mother's arms.

"I think you should take this with you."

Katherine was holding the gown out to her daughter.

"I could come with you, Lil; I'd really like to help you explain."

Just then, her father tapped on the door. "Good morning, Lil. How ya feeling this morning?"

"Good morning, Daddy." Lilly giggled, excited.

"What's going on in here?" he inquired, looking at them and baffled by the glowing dress.

"Wonderful magic," Katherine replied.

"It's the Magic Gown, Daddy! I brought it back from a magic place and now I have to tell the Finches about Tom! I'll be okay, Mommy, to tell them by myself, but thanks." Katherine smiled and nodded. "Okay," she said, hugging her daughter tightly.

Lilly skipped by her father, stopping to kiss him. "The world could use a little magic," he said. "Hey, when do I get to hear about this incredible adventure," he called to her, as she hurried down the stairs. "Mommy will tell you! I'll be back later, Daddy; I have to tell the Finches about Tom!"

Lilly was off to the Finches' with J following her, hopping from one snow covered branch to another along the way.

Lilly, carrying the dress, walked up the front porch steps. Jake, the dog, barked and Mary appeared at the door and opened it before she could knock.

"Lilly, I'm so glad to see you!"

"Hello, Mrs. Finch. I wanted to . . ."

"Wait until you see this! Come in, come in! Frank, Lilly's here!"

Frank Finch came into the hallway from the study.

"Hello, Mr. Finch."

"Well, hello there, young lady. You sure gave us some special roses for Christmas," said Mr. Finch.

"What do you mean?" asked Lilly.

"Come see for yourself."

Lilly followed him into the study, with Mrs. Finch and Jake behind her. There on the table with the geraniums was the rose plant pot. It was filled with the most beautiful colored blossoms: bright pink, deep red, butter yellow, orange-peach, and lavender with bright green leaves. The room was fragrant with the familiar scent of the rose garden in the Next Place.

"Tell us, Lilly, about where these marvelous flowers came from," Mary Finch coaxed her. "Mr. Finch and I think . . . well . . . we know this is a sign of some kind." She was almost too excited to speak.

"Yes," replied Lilly, "that's why I'm here. These are very special roses from a very special place. It's where Tom is."

Frank and Mary Finch stood speechless, looking at Lilly.

Lilly smiled and continued, "He wanted me to tell you that he's fine. I told him I would try and that I hoped you would believe me. But when I got home yesterday, I forgot everything until this morning, when I put on this magic dress."

The dress had a soft glow as Mary came closer and touched it. She took a deep breath. Frank moved to the couch and sat down, while Lilly stood in front of them. She began telling them from the beginning about the morning she caught the Shell of Great Fortune and

Mysterious Ways and how it
was the same morning Tom
followed the rare silver current of the crescent moon to
the Great Desert of Uncertainty, where he met Mr. H.
Myrrh. She told them about
Zara Bluewood and the blue
bedroom door, and so on.
When she came to the part
about Joseph, the blue elephant who was the moun-
tain man who brought Tom
to the orphanage, Mary
exclaimed, "It's true! That's
him! Remember, Frank, they
said he had a big blue coat,

dark skin, sparkling blue eyes and white hair!"

"That's him, the kindest king that ever was," said Lilly.

Mr. Finch put his arm around Mary and drew her closer to him.
"Tell us more about our Tom, Lilly."

Lilly continued with her story into the late afternoon, there was so
much more to tell, and at lunchtime she insisted they try the
Springtree honey from the little pouch Stee-Ven gave to her. They all
agreed it was the most delicious honey they had ever tasted!

THE END

LIKE THE BOOK?
Then you'll LOVE the art from it in these
LARGE COLOR POSTERS!

ONLY $14.95 EACH

MG-1: *First Door
—The Blue Door*
(from page 27)

MG-2: *Second Door
—The Carved Door*
(from page 37)

MG-3: *Third Door—The Crossed Swords*
(from page 44–45)

MG-5: *Fifth Door—The Next Place*
(from page 74–75)

MG-4: *Fourth Door
—The Springtree*
(from page 68)

MG-6: *Sixth Door—The Blue Elephant*
(from page 77)

*More posters
on next page*

MG-7: *Seventh Door—The Magic Cup*
(from page 78–79)

MG-8: Map: *The Land of Ten Kings and Roses*
(from page ii)

MG-9: *Mr. H. Myrrh —The Dragon King* (from page 48)

MG-10: *The Dancing Guitar* (from page 110)

MG-11: *The Blue Tree Forest* (from page 81)

MG-12: *The Red Tree Forest* (from page 82)

MG-13: *Moregrott and the Lacks* (from page 92)

All posters are a full 13" by 19" printed in vibrant colors on heavyweight, photo-quality, glossy paper and are suitable for framing of your choice as desired. For a larger view of these posters, please visit our Web sites at: **www.springtreepress.com** or **www.janinekimmel.com**

Order Form

POSTER #	TITLE	QUANTITY
MG-1	*First Door—The Blue Door*	
MG-2	*Second Door—The Carved Door*	
MG-3	*Third Door—The Crossed Swords*	
MG-4	*Fourth Door—The Springtree*	
MG-5	*Fifth Door—The Next Place*	
MG-6	*Sixth Door—The Blue Elephant*	
MG-7	*Seventh Door—The Magic Cup*	
MG-8	Map: *The Land of Ten Kings and Roses*	
MG-9	*Mr. H. Myrrh—The Dragon King*	
MG-10	*The Dancing Guitar*	
MG-11	*The Blue Tree Forest*	
MG-12	*The Red Tree Forest*	
MG-13	*Moregrott and the Lacks*	

SHIPPING CHART				
Posters Ordered	Charge	Total posters at $14.95 each =		
1 to 3	$ 4.95	New Jersey residents add 7% sales tax		
4 or more	$ 6.95	Shipping charge from chart		
		Order Total		

Make check or money order payable to: Spring Tree Press

☐ VISA or ☐ MasterCard# _____ Exp. _____

Signature _____ Date _____

Please print:

Name _____ Phone _____

Address _____

City _____ State _____ Zip _____

E-mail _____

Mail to: Spring Tree Press • P.O. Box 461 • Atlantic Highlands, NJ 07716

Cast of Characters

NOTE: The pronunciation guide included here works like this: The word to pronounce is shown in **bold** copy in parentheses (these curved marks) and is hyphenated (-) to show you the syllables. The syllables are just letters or words that rhyme with the syllables of the word you are trying to pronounce. Pronounce all the syllables together rapidly, but give the syllable that is all **CAPITALS** extra emphasis so that you hear it more than the others. If more than one syllable is all capitals, give them all equal emphasis.

ANDREW SEGOVIA: Lilly's father, a pianist and composer from Spain who met Lilly's mother when he lived in Brazil. (Pronounced **c-GO-v-uh**, rhyming with "see-go-be-huh.")

CAMEO: The ninth king, King of the Land of Ten Kings and Roses; he lives in the High Hibiscus Garden with Queen White Tears and can appear as a tropical eagle. (Pronounced **KAM-e-o**, rhyming with "ham-he-oh.")

CHIPZIES: Tic, Monk, Sandy, Red, and guitar-playing Robin, all shy, little, pine-nut farming, chipmunk people in the Sleeping Forest. (Pronounced **CHIP-zees**, rhyming with "gyp-sees"; if only one, it's **CHIP-z**, rhyming with "gyp-see.")

FRANK FINCH: Lilly's neighbor and adoptive father of Tom.

J: Lilly's pet blue jay.

JAKE: Tom's dog.

JOSEPH: A blue elephant who is the ruler of the Land of King Joseph and is known as "the kindest king that ever was."

KATHERINE KELLY SEGOVIA: Lilly's mother; botanical illustrator from the U.S. who met her husband while working in Brazil.

KING OF THE COLORFUL WIND: The king wind angel from the Realm of The Colorful Wind.

KING RUE: A cat person from the Red Tree Forest. (Pronounced **ROO**, like the last syllable in kangaroo.)

LACKS: Cruel eyeless creatures that grow out of the bones of greedy dragon's-gold thieves in the Great Desert of Uncertainty. (Pronounced **LAX**, rhyming with "tax"; if only one creature, it would be called a **LACK**, rhyming with "back.")

LILLY SEGOVIA: The daughter of Andrew Segovia and Katherine Kelly Segovia; age eleven.

MARY FINCH: Lilly's neighbor and adoptive mother of Tom.

MERCILES: A particularly vile Lack queen. (Pronounced **MER-c-less**, rhyming with "her-see-less"; if it's in the possessive form, say **MER-c-less-ez**, rhyming with "her-see-less-says.")

MIK: A cat person who accompanies King Rue. (Pronounced **MICK**, rhyming with "pick.")

MING-LI: A white moth and companion to Princess Anais. (Pronounced **MING-LEE**, rhyming with "bring-me.")

MOREGROTT: The horrible leader of the Lacks. (Pronounced **MORE-grot**, rhyming with "for-got.")

MR. H. MYRRH: A flying desert dragon who spits gold and is King of the Great Desert of Uncertainty. (Pronounced **MER**, rhyming with "her.")

MRS. LONDON: Lilly's neighbor and the lady who makes scones. (Pronounced **LUN-DUN**, rhyming with "fun-done."

NINAH: The snake-like Queen of the Shimmering World. (Pronounced **NEE-nuh**, rhyming with "knee-huh.")

NIZELLA: A beautiful fairy queen in the Sleeping Forest. (Pronounced **ni-ZEL-ah**, rhyming with "high-tell-ha.")

PRINCESS ANAIS: The princess from Beetle Island who wears the Magic Gown the Lacks are after. (Pronounced **ah-NAYS**, rhyming with "ah-grace; if it's in the possessive form, say **ah-NAYS-ez**, rhyming with "ah-grace-says.")

QUEEN OF THE COLORFUL WIND: The queen wind angel from the Realm of the Colorful Wind.

STEE-VEN: The Dancing Tree Man in the Springtree who guides people to the Next Place. (Pronounced **STEE-VEN**, rhyming with "be-when.")

THE FISH: An orange and gold messenger fish who travels in the beak of a white seagull named Tu.

THE ROCK: A talking rock lying between the Butterfly Cliffs and the Sleeping Forest.

THERESA: A talking red butterfly from the Realm of the Colorful Wind who "appears whenever change is in the air." (Pronounced **ta-REE-sa**, rhyming with "ha-tea-huh.")

TOM FINCH: Lilly's neighbor and the adopted son of Mary and Frank Finch; age twelve.

TU: A dream guardian white seagull who transports The Fish. (Pronounced **TWO**, rhyming with "too" and "to.")

VIKTOR: The tiger guardian of the Hidden Lake of Ker-Es who was transformed from Moregrott the Lack. (Pronounced **VIK-ter**, rhyming with "tricked-her.")

WHITE TEARS: Queen of the Land of Ten Kings and Roses; she lives in the High Hibiscus Garden with King Cameo and can appear as a tropical eagle.

ZARA BLUEWOOD: The blue swan from the Blue Tree Forest who tells Lilly to be ready for her journey to a place of magic. (Pronounced **ZAR-ah**, rhyming with "star-huh.")

Gazetteer & Glossary

NOTE: The pronunciation guide included here works like this: The word to pronounce is shown in **bold** copy in parentheses (these curved marks) and is hyphenated (-) to show you the syllables. The syllables are just letters or words that rhyme with the syllables of the word you are trying to pronounce. Pronounce all the syllables together rapidly, but give the syllable that is all **CAPITALS** extra emphasis so that you hear it more than the others. If more than one syllable is all capitals, give them all equal emphasis.

BEETLE ISLAND: An island in the Silver Sea of Silence shaped like the Shell of Great Fortune and Mysterious Ways and where the Silver Water Falls and the Enchanted Fruit Forest are; the place where Princess Anais grew up. (Pronounced **BEET-ul**, rhyming with John Lennon, the "Beatle.")

BLUE TREE FOREST: A forest of bright blue trees and the home of Zara Bluewood; the Deep Blue River runs through the center of this forest.

BUTTERFLY CLIFFS: Steep cliff walls made of red and yellow butterflies that lie before the Sleeping Forest.

CANYONLANDS: An in-between land; a strange place where the magic is so strong that it is tricky; it lies between the Sleeping Forest and the Seven Jeweled Mountains of Ker-Es. (Pronounced **CAN-yun-lands**, rhyming with "man-son-plans.")

CHIPZIES: Shy little pine-nut farming chipmunk people in the Sleeping Forest. (Pronounced **CHIP-zees**, rhyming with "gypsees"; if only one, it's **CHIP-z**, rhyming with "gyp-see.")

CLAY PIT CREEK: The tidal creek by Lilly's house in New Jersey where she kayaks.

CRACK OF DESPAIR: Located in the Great Desert of Uncertainty and one way to the Lack city of Grott. (Pronounced **di-SPER**, rhyming with "this-bear.")

CUP: A large golden cup found on King Joseph's table and filled with the water from the Deep Blue River in the Blue Tree Forest.

DANCING GUITAR: A tiny guitar played by Robin, one of the Chipzies in the Sleeping Forest. (Pronounced **gi-TAR**, rhyming with "get-far.")

DARK GREEN OCEAN OF FORTUNE: The green body of water where the great green sharks swim; it lies north of the Silver Sea of Silence and extends to the jagged steep cliffs of the Wild Land of Skree. (Pronounced **FOR-chun**, rhyming with "chore-done.")

DEEP BLUE RIVER: A river running through the Blue Tree Forest.

DIFFERENT KIND OF ROAD: A road one must find to the Springtree.

DRAGON'S GOLD: Formed from the golden dripping saliva of royal magical flying desert dragons.

ENCHANTED CEDAR STUMP: The favorite meeting place of the fairies in the center of the Sleeping Forest. A place to find your direction. (Pronounced **in-CHAN-ted**, rhyming with "he-plant-ed.")

ENCHANTED FRUIT FOREST: Located on Beetle Island.

FIFTH DOOR: Doorway to the Next Place, the place of one's own creation.

FIRST DOOR: The blue door to Peach Sand Cove when the time is right.

FOURTH DOOR: The door in the Springtree in the heart of the Land of Ten Kings and Roses.

GAZETTEER: A dictionary of geographical places. (Pronounced **ga-za-TEER**, rhyming with "jazz-I-hear.")

GLOSSARY: A dictionary of the words that are specific to a particular subject. (Pronounced **GLOSS-ah-re**, rhyming with "boss-I-be.")

GOLDEN OCEAN OF MYSTERY: The mysterious shimmering golden-like body of water lying east of the Land of Ten Kings and Roses. (Pronounced **MIS-ta-re**, rhyming with "his-car-see.")

GREAT DESERT OF UNCERTAINTY: The home of the Lacks and Mr. H. Myrrh. (Pronounced **DES-urt**, rhyming with "my-shirt"; **un-SUR-ten-te**, rhyming with "fun-fur-spent-he.")

GROTT: A dismal underground city in the land of the Lacks. (Pronounced **GROT**, rhyming with "rot.")

HAIR ROPE: Made by Mr. H. Myrrh of the hair from dead people and found lying next to the Well of Unfathomable Suffering.

HIDDEN LAKE OF KER-ES: A beautiful glistening lake encircled by the Seven Jeweled Mountains of Ker-Es. (Pronounced **kur-S**, rhyming with "fur-mess.")

HIGH HIBISCUS GARDEN: The home of King Cameo and White Tears. (Pronounced **hi-BIS-kus**, rhyming with "why-this-bus.")

LACKS: Cruel eyeless creatures that grow out of the bones of greedy dragon's-gold thieves in the Great Desert of Uncertainty. (Pronounced **LAX**, rhyming with "tax"; if only one creature, it would be called a **LACK**, rhyming with "back.")

LADY SCARAB: Princess Anais's sailboat made of enchanted fruit-wood with a beetle embroidered on the bright yellow sail. (Pronounced **SKER-ub**, rhyming with "scare-club.")

LAND OF TEN KINGS AND ROSES: The home of Princess Anais and the Magic Gown.

LAVENDER TUNDRA: The land where a Different Kind of Road is. (Pronounced **LAV-in-der**, rhyming with "have-skin-fur.")

MAGIC GOWN: An ancient magical dress from the Realm of the Colorful Wind.

NEXT PLACE: The place of one's own creation reached from the Springtree.

NOJOKE RIVER: The green-water river in the Wild Land of Skree that runs from the Dark Green Ocean of Fortune past the Zumbrogarwan Mountains to the Seven Jeweled Mountains of Ker-Es. (Pronounced **NO-JOKE**, rhyming with "go-broke.")

PEACH SAND COVE: The place in the Land of Ten Kings and Roses where the first door takes you when the time is right.

REALM OF THE COLORFUL WIND: Home of the King and Queen of the Colorful Wind and known as the place of endings and true beginnings; the origin of the Magic Gown. (Pronounced **RELM**, rhyming with "elm.")

RED TREE FOREST: A forest of bright red trees where the magic gets very strong; home of the cat people, King Rue and Mik.

RUBYROCK FALLS: A beautiful waterfall made of ruby jewels and located at the far reaches of the High Hibiscus Garden. (Pronounced **REW-BE-ROK**, rhyming with "do-he-knock.")

RED WOODEN BOX: A box carved from wood of the Red Tree Forest in the Land of Ten Kings and Roses and containing magic seeds.

SECOND DOOR: The carved wooden arched door to the Colorful Wind.

SEVEN JEWELED MOUNTAINS OF KER-ES: The circle of seven snow-covered, peaked majestic mountains north of the Wild Land of Skree and west of the Sleeping Forest. (See Hidden Lake of **Ker-Es** for pronunciation.)

SEVENTH DOOR: A doorway that appears after drinking the Deep Blue River water from the cup.

SHELL OF GREAT FORTUNE AND MYSTERIOUS WAYS: A seashell whose origin is the shallow silver waters around Beetle Island in the Land of Ten Kings and Roses. (Pronounced **mis-STER-re-us**, rhyming with "this-deer-see-us.")

SHIMMERING WORLD: An enchanted illuminated underwater place. (Pronounced **SHIM-ur-ING**, rhyming with "trim-her-wing.")

SILVER CURRENT OF THE CRESCENT MOON: A rare silver current that appears in a river or ocean during the time of a charmed crescent moon. (Pronounced **KRES-unt**, rhyming with "dress-hunt.")

SILVER SEA OF SILENCE: The body of water in which Beetle Island is located.

SILVER WATER FALLS: Located on Beetle Island.

SIXTH DOOR: An unusual doorway leading to the Land of King Joseph.

SLEEPING FOREST: An ancient forest that has fallen asleep; home of the talking rock, the Chipzies, Nizella and the enchanted cedar stump.

SPIRALED SNAKE STAFF: The protecting staff of Cameo, the ninth king. (Pronounced **SPI-ruld**, rhyming with "tire-rolled.")

SPRINGTREE: The point of no return on the Different Kind of Road.

SPRINGTREE HONEY: Delicious celestial honey made from the Springtree.

STAR-GAZER: Tom Finch's wooden motorboat.

THIRD DOOR: The double doors with crossed light blue swords to The Great Desert of Uncertainty

WELL OF UNFATHOMABLE SUFFERING: Located in the Great Desert of Uncertainty and leading to many places depending upon the visitor's intention. (Pronounced **UN-FA-THA-ma-bul**, rhyming with "un-gather-my-wool.")

WILD LAND OF SKREE: The land to the north of the Dark Green Ocean of Fortune which will be renamed the Land of Ker-Es when the tenth king arrives. (When the letters "Skree" are rearranged, it spells "Ker-Es.") (Pronounced **SKRE**, rhyming with "gee")

ZUMBROGARWAN MOUNTAINS: Four steep mountains that stand along the Nojoke River in the Wild Land of Skree like noble guardians. (Pronounced **zum-bro-GAR-when**, rhyming with "some-old-car-men.")